In The Land of Keldarra...

Emelyse and Bergas

Nathalie M.L. Römer

Emerentsia Publications
Marielundsvägen 9c
711 95 Gusselby
Sweden
emerentsiabooks.com

Ordering Information:

Orders by U.S. trade bookstores and wholesalers. Please contact Ingram: One Ingram Blvd., La Vergne, TN 37086 • 615.793.5000 or visit www.ingramcontent.com.

Independently printed as a Swedish publication.

Interior design and layout by Emerentsia Publications.

Official Website:
nathaliemlromer.com

Official Facebook Page:
facebook.com/nathaliemlromer

Official Twitter Account:
twitter.com/nmlromer

Book website: nathaliemlromer.com/emelyse-and-bergas

For my loving partner Anders.

Emelyse

CHAPTER ONE

Emelyse looks on nervously as her mother Anayra packs the last of her daughter's clothing into the haversack. She glances out of the window, and she sees the sky becoming lighter by the minute. If they don't leave soon, there's a risk for the guardsmen to start their daytime patrol.

The requirement is for Anayra to deliver her daughter to the Temple of the Hidden *before* the sun rises above the mountain flanking the city to the east, and this is now perhaps less than half an hour away. The walk to the old thief's stairs they plan to use as a means for Emelyse to leave Damrachia is a good fifteen to twenty minutes walk from their house, and that's if they're quick. And although the distance isn't that great, the danger of discovery is.

The front door opening, then closing, followed by a soft cough, alerts both women that Dargu has arrived. He's going to assist in the carrying of the haversack, ahead of them so the two women won't stand out as they walk through the city and in case any see them. He also knows the hidden paths in the city, which many in the city avoid.

"Mother, you're taking too long--" Emelyse's voice sounds nervous.

"I'm almost ready. The travel over the Upper Plains is long, and you need to be adequately prepared--" Anayra replies sharply.

Emelyse glances up at her mother. She shows shock. She's scared, and her mother's apparent anger doesn't make her feel any happier, nor does it ease their impending parting.

"I'm sorry, Emsy--" Anayra says, when she notices the upset on her daughter's face.

The name her mother calls her by brings a fleeting, nervous smile on Emelyse's face. It's a name her mother hasn't used for the last ten years, mostly on the insistence of Emelyse herself. But now the name feels like it offers her *hope*, and a measure of safety. For a moment Emelyse wants to feel like she's a nine-year-old again, sitting on her mother's lap, to listen to her mother's many retellings, and her beautiful singing. She knows those days would *never* happen again. Her skill had manifested itself almost ten years ago, and it's then that her mother had taught her strange things. They never left the house. Especially *not* after her skill showed itself. And when it *did,* her mother became very sad…

Emelyse cannot tell her mother how she's feeling right now, or it will cause her to feel more worry.

"Are you ladies ready?" Dargu pokes his head around the room's doorway.

"Yes, almost--" Now Anayra's rich youthful voice is filled with the emotions she's been denying herself for the previous fifteen days. Her voice suddenly sounds so much older because of it.

Dargu looks at Anayra. He understands her pain. He knows his own daughter, Errysa, may get called to Temple of the Hidden. Anayra's daughter needs to go *now*. Errysa is nine years younger than Emelyse, and the two girls grew up almost like sisters. Dargu knows his daughter *will* miss Emelyse deeply after she leaves the city.

Emelyse gets up and puts on her coat and fastens it at the front with two cords.

"I'm ready--" she says resolutely.

Anayra hands the haversack to Dargu, showing a momentary hesitation looking directly into the man's eyes. He looks down at her and nods affirmatively, even though she didn't state the question she needs to ask. Her eyes betray some panic, and she squeezes her lips tight together to control the emotions welling up in her, mostly so she can hide it from her daughter.

Dargu takes the haversack, and without saying a word he turns and descends the stairs. He pauses when he reaches the bottom and turns.

"Follow in five minutes," he says quietly. Before Anayra can say anything in response, he paces quickly to the front door, and a moment later he is gone.

Anayra glances at Emelyse and sees her stare blankly forward, biting her lower lip to stop herself from crying.

"Emsy, you know we *need* to do this--" Anayra walks to Emelyse, putting both arms around the younger woman in a comforting embrace. She holds her daughter without speaking. Words can never take Emelyse's pain away, so they say none. Emelyse has only been a woman for a few days, becoming one in a hastily arranged Second Rites ritual, which was sparse in its execution compared to usual times.

After a number of minutes, Anayra gently lets go of her daughter, and she takes Emelyse's face in both hands and lifts her face up. Mother and daughter look each other directly in the eyes.

"Travel west over the mountains. Once you're past the first of the watchtowers and past the ravine, you'll be in *safer* lands--"

Emelyse nods solemnly.

Anayra picks her own coat off the bed and puts it on in a rush. She takes hold of her daughter's hand, and slowly both walk down the stairs. Once downstairs, Anayra opens the front door and looks both ways for any passersby. There are none.

"Let us hurry," she whispers, "Dargu waits--"

Both women step onto the street and both glance up to the sky. No sun is visible yet, so there's some time to spare.

Silently side by side the two women walk, and at the end of the street, they turn right. If Anayra had been delivering her daughter to the Temple of the Hidden as instructed, they'd have turned left here. Haste is now their motivation to quicken their step even more, but occasionally Anayra does slow them when other people are near.

"Anayra--This way!"

Anayra's heart skips a beat when she hears Dargu's voice come from an unfamiliar passage. It's not the place they'd agreed on.

"There are guards up ahead. It seems they're checking everyone," Dargu hisses. "Come this way now before they see either of you--"

Mother and daughter glance only once at each other, then they turn sharply and follow Dargu into the dark passage. They know Dargu is a lot more familiar with the old parts of the city. He never speaks about how he knows this, but Anayra always guesses it was the *same* reason *she* knows much of the future.

One aspect of that future she hides even from *him* even though she trusts Dargu is the vision she's been seeing of a golden-haired girl riding a wolf…

CHAPTER TWO

Emelyse's heart pounds as another group of soldiers passes them. She recognises *who* they are, and knows that those inside the Temple of the Hidden have sent them out to round up girls like *her* who either are refusing to obey the command to go there or, like her, are trying to escape.

She knows from being told by her mother that this is *one* reason she's never allowed to walk the streets.

The Elder in the mysterious dark building in the centre of the city is the one issuing the command and always at the most unexpected timings. Emelyse is certain that the woman somehow has to know what goes on in the city; each Elder who came before her possessed the same ability.

She'd heard the many retellings about how the *first* of these Elders came from the west and betrayed those who were running the Temple. They had shown Emelyse the old building where the betrayal started…

"Your destiny lies elsewhere. Your destiny is to bring the message of warning to those who need it--"

Emelyse never asks *who* the people mentioned are, but as she shares her mother's skill of foresight, she's certain that her mother is sending her somewhere *specific,* where she can meet these unknown people. She *also* has seen a vision of a girl on the back of a wolf, and for a reason unknown to her, there's something reassuring about seeing *that* image.

She feels a hand on her arm and looking up she sees Dargu's concerned eyes looking down at her.

"Have courage," he says. Emelyse nods. Though she doesn't

know how she'd find the courage to make a journey that *any* man would call foolhardy. And she's doing this journey at barely past her Second Rites.

Emelyse looks back towards the street where shouts can be heard. She sees three soldiers pulling a girl along the street. A woman, who seems a bit younger than her own mother, screams at the soldiers, and despite their strength to pull the girl away from her, she lands a few hard blows on the face of one soldier. He's dazed a moment, then she's knocked flat on the ground from a blow from him.

Emelyse quickly places her two hands over her mouth to make sure she doesn't scream out. She feels a hand against her chest and Dargu's voice from far away.

"No, we can't. If we help, they'll know we're here. We need to *go*, Anayra--"

Anayra stares hard at the man beside her and then sees he also keeps a firm grip on her daughter. She knows that he understands that not just she, but also Emelyse, wants to help the fallen woman. She nods and feels the grip relax, but it doesn't let go.

Almost forcefully, Dargu pulls mother and daughter onto their feet and walks through the alleyway towards where their destination is located. The two women have a hard time keeping up with the much taller man with his long strides.

Only minutes later, they're at the small opening in the western wall which has served many as a means to escape from the city. Today, it will serve in that task *one* last time. It will be *too* dangerous to send *any* others through this means after today.

They stand for a few minutes just staring at each other. Dargu gives the haversack to Emelyse, who now looks wide-eyed in fear in each direction. "I must go--" she whispers.

"Yes, she *needs* to go--" Dargu urges.

Anayra pulls Emelyse towards her in a tight embrace, "Be watchful of where you go, my daughter--"

"I will be, Mam."

Anayra pushes Emelyse away from herself, and she looks at her daughter's face for a long time. She knows she'll never see her daughter again in her lifetime. Her heart hopes for safety for her daughter, even though they both know that the trek through Upper Plains is virtually impossible to do on foot.

"Remember everything I said."

Emelyse nods.

"Now go, my daughter. Make sure you're not seen in the valley between the city and the mountains in the west."

"I won't be seen."

"She needs to go, Anayra," Dargu says with increased urgency in his voice.

Anayra gives Emelyse a last hug, then turns her forcefully and pushes her towards the narrow opening in the wall. Emelyse glances one more time over her shoulder before she steps through the breach. She clambers over the stones and is startled when a few minutes later she hears the sounds of falling stone behind her. When the rising dust settles, she sees the breach closed with rubble and rocks. Her way back is closed off. She *is* the last to leave…

"Farewell, Mam," she whispers, "I'll return if I can--and I'll carry this message you gave me with me until I meet the *ones* it's meant for. Just as you instructed--"

Emelyse turns walks at a fast pace through the undergrowth that borders the city on this side of the city. She heads in a somewhat northerly direction, past the high rocky outcrop flanking the city on the west side. She glances up at the plateau where she and Errysa had often played. Errysa said she'd try to be there to wave goodbye, but her absence means that her father has forbidden her to go outside.

I guess they're right about the city being too dangerous to be in now. I hope Errysa will be alright--

Emelyse walks, but she constantly looks up at the walls just in case soldiers are there. From within the city, she can hear the screams shows more girls are being gathered for their ominous trek to the dark building standing in the central part of the city. She hears a nearby scream and hides under a rock overhang and waits. She closes her eyes, and her mind again sees the girl being dragged away while her mother lies knocked to the ground by a blow.

I need to hurry so they don't come looking out here for me.

She looks at the landscape ahead.

If I can reach the woodland across the vale before the sun reaches over the crest of the eastern mountain range, I can get away unseen by all.

As she walks at the fast pace, every sound coming from the city behind her makes her bolt for the nearest rock to hide, but the intensity of the sounds diminish as she gets further away, and then seems to end. Before her lies the untamed wilderness of Upper Plains with its own challenges…

CHAPTER THREE

Emelyse stops running. She glances towards Damrachia. At this distance, it seems small, almost insignificant. Emelyse reaches to her cheek when she feels it wet. "I can't get upset," she chides herself, "Mother won't be!" Emelyse sighs. She doesn't know *what* the journey will bring her.

She remembers the years of her mother telling her to be watchful of her surroundings, and now that caution makes her jumpy of every sound she hears around her.

I need to be strong for this journey. I just need to be strong--

It's the same words she'd always say to a much younger Errysa, who doesn't yet understand how dangerous the city could be. Emelyse's shoulders slump as she realises that she won't see her friend - almost like a sister - ever again.

"Please *keep* her safe, and *try* to send her to *wherever* I'm going," she whispers.

However, deep down she knows already that isn't possible. The situation in the city is getting worse by the hour, and they removed the means to send people away. Errysa is far too young for the journey to be undertaken.

Emelyse climbs the first footpath, which leads to a small field below the mountain range. The climb up is tedious, mostly because of her large haversack. They had given her a man's haversack so she can alter her appearance and let people *assume* she's a boy on an errand. Emelyse looks for a place where she can change her clothing. It will help her not to be recognised. She sees a thick bush and heads to it.

She feels self-conscious as she removes her skirt, shirt and underdress, and proceeds to put on some trousers that once belonged to Dargu at a much younger age, then she puts on a thick woollen sweater which she fastens tight at her waist to make sure it hides that she's, in fact, a female. After that, she puts on a coat given to her by her mother.

From the haversack, she grabs a knife and after a moment's hesitation cuts off her long flowing hair just below the nape. Emelyse digs a hole in the soil and buries the bundle of hair as her mother has instructed her to do. There are so many things her mother had instructed. Emelyse is having a hard time remembering it all now.

Those instructions guide her actions more because the emotions left her numb.

Once the hole is deep enough, Emelyse pushes the hair bundle in it. She refills it, gets upright and pushes on the place where the hair was buried just moments earlier with her foot to make sure it's secure and hidden.

Emelyse glances in all directions to make sure she truly is alone. Emelyse frowns when she realises how *still* her surroundings are. She can feel her heart pounding, and her forehead feels clammy.

No, not now.

Although her mother has instructed her how to prevent these awakenings when they want to manifest themselves, she still has trouble preventing it when one wants to show itself. Emelyse shuts her eyes and concentrates on her breathing. The surrounding stillness becomes more prominent than a darkness enters her mind.

Emelyse opens her eyes and realises she no longer sees the surrounding forest. She sees a city. An unfamiliar foreign city. She sees a girl walking through a street in a pensive mood. It's not any person she recognises. Something about the girl *still* feels familiar like she should know the girl from something… or somewhere. The girl has shoulder-length blond hair, and blue eyes, a long flowing dress, but the surroundings are like nothing Emelyse has ever seen before.

She watches the girl walking along the street. Then arrive at a building where more people stand waiting. A confrontation seems to happen between the girl and some others. Emelyse feels panic rise when she sees a scene that seems so familiar. But here there are no sad faces, no one seems in fear, and there are no soldiers present either.

Emelyse frowns. It's certain she is doing an awakening of some sort. But to see something so unfamiliar… She looks at the people she guesses are the *Elders* in this Temple. *Something* about the old woman overlooking the procedures is so familiar but, she tries Emelyse can't figure out what it might be. *Who* else has piercing green eyes such as *she…?*

A moment later a black fog covers over the scene and Emelyse sits rubbing her temples from a headache she'd developed from the strain of stopping the awakening. She leans forward and groans loudly. She expels one cursing she'd heard Dargu do so often.

I need to learn to control this and fast, or the journey will be even more dangerous, she thinks. *What if I'm like this and someone finds me?*

Emelyse looks again in every direction. She again hears the sounds of the animals and birds around her and realises that the apparent silence earlier is nothing more than a trick played on her by her emerging skill as a Caller.

If Mam saw me like this now, I'd disappoint her. She didn't spend so much time teaching me what I need to know for me to fail only a half day after leaving. The girl I saw. I'm certain that's in the future. I remember Mam telling me that certain awakenings happen at the moment of birth…

Emelyse straightens up and feels like she realises something amazing. That it's possible that she did an awakening told about in the ancient books of the old Temple of Damrachia. In them it's stated not just once but *many* times that there are certain turning points in history where past and future *converge*, and if a person of importance for altering the future to a new direction is born that a strong Caller can see a vision of their future at the moment of birth…

"Could it be?" Emelyse wonders. "Could I've seen the *coming* of such a person as described in the books? I remember reading that such people are *only* born every few hundred years, and they could either be a force of good or a force that can spell disaster to the world. According to Mam, the one who built the Temple of the Hidden had been one who'd spelt disaster to the world. Dammit, *where* is there a Preserver when you need *one*…?"

CHAPTER FOUR

"Four days of walking and I've *yet* to reach Upper Plains," Emelyse mutters.

She glances up when a moment later something wet splatters on her face. "Oh, right--So *now* we need to add *rain* to the mixture of providence," Emelyse calls out. "Alright, I *may* be a crappy *Caller*, still learning my skill, but no one taught me the skill of predicting the damned weather."

Emelyse looks around and sees something that might be a small cave in a clearing in the woodland. *I guess that will have to do until this rain goes away--*

She clambers into the cave and feels an immediate discomfort being inside the enclosed space. Emelyse curls herself into a ball, and rocks back and forth while her eyes dart back and forth.

Something terrible will happen here. But I don't know what, and I don't want to do another awakening so soon--

Emelyse feels tears well up. Now that she isn't travelling for a time, her emotions get the better of her, and suddenly she can't do anything but cry. Something wet her cheeks through in minutes. Emelyse cries, and after a few minutes, she hiccups as her sobbing becomes almost uncontrollable. After about thirty minutes it subsides, and Emelyse feels better.

"I *need* to get control--I *need* to get control--" Emelyse repeats over and over.

Emelyse opens her haversack, and from it retrieves a small pouch containing dried meat. She also pulls a small bowl from her haversack and places the meat in it. She pours some water from her water bag over it, then rises from the sandy soil to get some wood for a fire.

Emelyse glances first in all directions to ensure she's still alone, then cautiously walks around picking up as much wood as possible before dashing in a sprint back to the small cave. As she enters, the discomfort re-enters her mind.

Emelyse makes a simple meat and broth mixture, which she partially eats with her fingers and partially drinks it down. It's some of her mother's roasted ailep hound meat that she loves so much. The memory of meals eaten with her mother brings a momentary smile to her face.

Most of the memories of her time at home are good; her mother always shielded her from the genuine horrors of what went on in Damrachia and always stressed to her daughter that it possibly best she did everything to forget it all.

"I'll forget it," Emelyse mutters, "No matter what, no one *will* know who I was *or* where I came from--"

But as she says the words, Emelyse knows that she also *still* has a message to deliver.

I wonder why mother thinks a man and a woman will come to me for help, Emelyse wonders, *And mother, why did you believe that it links the birthing of my child to it--*

There are too many questions with *no* answers right now. She sighs…

She knows her destiny differs from what she'd always dreamt about. Emelyse looks into an easterly direction towards the place, where the *only* people she really cares about are located.

Be safe, little sister, be safe--

She *knows* that her mother and Dargu will do everything they can to make sure her friend Errysa *is* alright. However, every time Emelyse had looked at her lifelong friend, she'd felt that something terrible will happen with her friend. That she'll *never* see her again, nor be able to say a proper goodbye, because of what 'they're going to *do* to her'. She denies herself the reason to speculate on who the 'they' in her thoughts might be.

Now she's already far from that friend, and she knows she won't see that friend ever again.

Emelyse looks up. She hears a sound outside the small cave she's in: *Who's out there?*

She looks around for something to use as a weapon, but Emelyse finds nothing other than loose gravel and small twigs.

What's out there?

Emelyse feels the earlier panic rise once more, but then she giggles uncontrollably in the next moment when a tiny creature enters the cave. Somehow, a baby vole has got itself separated from the rest of its nest companions, and has scurried its way into the tiny cave that has been occupied by a young frightened woman, barely an adult yet, who has become one by necessity.

Emelyse's giggle stops the tiny animal in its tracks. The animal freezes in place when it hears an unfamiliar sound. It sits transfixed and sniffs the air. Emelyse sees how scared the creature is, and it gives her a new perspective of her own situation.

I'm like that young vole. I'm a young person all alone in a world, which I don't understand or which I cannot trust without the guidance I need to learn to live in it. But unlike that small animal, I have the means to learn--

In a slow-motion, she stretches her hand out.

If that youngling can learn to trust instinct to come to me, then I know I learn to trust my source of instinct. I know I can learn to trust the Awakenings--

She waits. She holds her breath and waits even more. But then smiles when she sees motion. The vole twitches its nose a few times, lands on its front legs it had raised off the ground and scurries forward about a half pace, just short of reaching the woman's hand. Then it lifts its body off the ground and sniffs again.

Come here, little one, come here--

The little creature lifts up again and as it gets even closer, Emelyse feels herself straining to try to will the baby vole to reach her hand. Moments later, she feels a tiny wet nose touch her middle finger, then as fast the animal rushes away. Emelyse is annoyed for a moment but then hears a sound that she recognises as an adult vole.

Obviously, the mother calling her youngling to her--

The experience has lifted her mind from despair to a measure of happy feeling again.

She smiles.

Next time I'm having an awakening, I won't fight it, but let it take me to whatever future it wants to show me.

Emelyse doesn't know *yet* that the next awakening will start changing her entire outlook on life. She doesn't know *yet* that it will prove to her how correct she is with her earlier assessments that the awakenings she'd experienced in Damrachia are those of a girl with her own destiny to fulfil in the world they live in.

That the vision she saw of a woman on the back of a wolf will become a reality in her own future…

CHAPTER FIVE

Emelyse listens. She's certain she has heard the same sounds several times before during her long trek through the eastern part of Upper Plains; the vast expanse of mountains that acts as a natural barrier between the northern ocean and the vast steppes of the south. The sound she hears has an eerie feeling to it, and it reminds the young woman of some retellings told in Damrachia about possible ghostly apparitions that *some* claim to be the spirits of the northern invaders…

I'm certain that's not a true retelling. It was told by the first one to those who followed her into the evil ways of the Temple and who created the Temple of the Hidden with her--But Emelyse can't stop her apprehension from growing stronger.

Seeing the massive dark shape of a building to the west doesn't help either. Its shape and general outline very much reminded her of the Temple of the Hidden, and the building gives her a feeling of foreboding. Even if she's still several weeks from arriving at it. The other thing giving her a similar feeling of foreboding is the sounds she hears in the wind--*wolf song*. She'd been told by Dargu to be wary of these beasts, and he'd claimed that hearing *them* either means she's near the wild wolves of Upper Plains *or* that she's nearing those who use them for riding.

Emelyse remembers giggling when Dargu had said this. But then she'd stopped giggling when he'd looked stern at her. From his expression, she'd known he isn't narrating one of his many entertaining retellings, but something serious. She knows she'll miss his retellings. It occurs then to her that almost every retelling had had some other meaning to them. When he'd told her about the northern invaders, he'd told a lot of what he knew of a city far to the west, which is an old harbour city where the northern invaders came first, and where ultimately they got driven from the land, and that after another battle that happened not too far from here.

What did Dargu call the battle again? Wasn't it called Battle of Nightmare Ridge--? I wonder who thought up that awful name. I don't think I want to go there. That's probably where the retelling of ghosts of northern invaders originates from. I do wonder who won--

Somewhere directly north of where Emelyse walks, the battle had happened--it happened close to fifteen hundred years ago when the *Wolf Masters*, the sworn protectors and defenders of Keldarra, swore allegiance to its safety and protection, and *not* to their later fate and destiny as the attackers of the land.

Emelyse stops when she hears wolf song in the distance. It seems to come from somewhere south of here. It's very distant, still, but it's definitely closer now than she'd heard it a few days earlier.

I should have stayed in the cave a few more days to rest more--

"I'm not scared," she blurts out in a loud voice, but she flinches when her voice echoes back at her through the desolate landscape.

No, Emelyse, you need to be brave now--Be brave--

She increases her pace, constantly looking over her shoulder, like some*one* or some*thing* is following her right now. Her awakenings, her emerging skill as a Caller, gives her a heightened sense of foreboding, and Emelyse feels that *soon* she'll know answers to some of her questions that keep invading her mind.

There's a city where it all began, it's also where it must end--

Emelyse knows she has seen those words in one of the ancient books she read when she visited the ancient first Temple in Damrachia with her mother. *Her mother insisted--*

"How can all this end if we cannot even rid ourselves of the Temple of the Hidden?" she'd asked her mother. Her mother's reply had been as cryptic as the words in the book are, "We can when we have knowledge of the past again. The woman who brings that will be the one who'll also unravel all that's been happening for so long, but she brings another who'll unravel that which will cause it to happen again--"

Emelyse remembers Dargu's face across her at the table who'd seemed to smirk at the words, and almost seemed to copy her in his snickering, which was an imitation of her giggle. It's after that when she never laughs anymore whenever he narrated retellings; it's then that she'd paid very close attention to them as well.

Especially after my Awakening--

The memories of those younger years hurt--now more than ever before--and over the preceding season since leaving, Emelyse often wished that she could just turn and go back home. But every time she looks east, she'd hear her mother's last words to her, *"Remember everything I said."*

She *will* remember, and she will also heed her mother's warning.

In the west lies the city, Dargu had told her about. He'd told her *also* that the woman leading its Temple *once* came to Damrachia to warn Anayra, and one *other,* of the danger that will come again from the west. She'd warned that only that other woman's daughter, a woman whose name Dargu kept from Emelyse, will stop that coming danger. Emelyse remembers still when he'd recited the words apparently spoken.

"A girl is going to enter a Temple in the west many years from now, if there's no guidance for her there, the one who means to betray us all is going to attack here and set in motion events that'll lead to a new time of enslavement. But this time that threat doesn't come from outside, but from these shores. Your daughter can open that girl's eyes, and then she and a man from the enemy will each play a role in bringing all this to an end. Your daughter, Emelyse, also has a role in this. She'll guide that girl to me--"

The day after Dargu told her the words, her first Awakening came. Emelyse remembers waking up screaming, and she remembers how moments after she'd had her mother's arms around her. *When* Dargu arrived at their house, she's still uncertain of, but soon after they moved to a different house. After that day, she never walked the streets of Damrachia anymore...

CHAPTER SIX

The height of the watchtower overwhelms Emelyse as she looks up. To her, it seems to reach so far up that it's touching the low clouds above Upper Plains. The damage she can see at its top tells her that the building probably stood at least three or four floors higher.

She looks ahead along the narrow road. *She'll come from 'that way' when she needs to travel to where I came from--*

It's another of those random thoughts that now keep popping up more and more frequently into Emelyse's mind as the will of the awakening process grows ever stronger inside her learning centre.

She'll be able to see this building's past--

Emelyse doesn't have a name for the girl she sees in her awakenings. It's someone with blond hair, startling blue eyes, and she's certain there's a connection to the girl because she always reaches up with her hand to a bulge in the upper part of her tunic. When this memory of the awakening enters Emelyse's mind, she shudders knowing she does this exact motion with her own hand towards where she keeps her own similar gem. A gem she now carries in a small pocket she has sewn in the inside of her underskirt.

No person will ever know I possess such a gem, and as I'll have a son, I won't have anyone to pass it onto either--

They also conditioned Emelyse to know that the gem which the unknown girl will call Stone of Truth, is never to be given to or to be used by males. Her gem is called Stone of Calling, and one day she'd simply bury it somewhere so no one will find it after she dies.

I can do it now, and then perhaps this skill will simply go away--

Emelyse frowns. She wonders why she keeps getting such

conflicting thoughts about her skill. She should be proud to be one of those to possess it, but then she realises too that the reason she isn't proud is, because of the danger *her skill* brings to the lives of those similar to herself: any who are found to experience an Awakening are always immediately singled out to go to the Temple of the Hidden, and to do *something* there. What that *something* is, that's what apparently Dargu, her mother, and others are fighting against, and had fought against for many generations now.

Emelyse knows that her own mother differs from others. She seems to understand the past *better* than most: she also seems to know about the future. Her mother apparently had been subjected to the *same* shielding as she subjected her daughter to. We never found her skill out…

Perhaps the shielding has been going on for as long as the problems have existed--

"I wonder if the *first* one caused all the problems at home, or that the northern invaders did that?" Emelyse mumbles; unless she somehow can learn to see the past, it's a question she'd never gain answers to.

She'll know--I'll make sure she understands what's at stake. However much I don't like what happened to me, I shouldn't deny my role in all this. There's so much more at stake than just one person's life. Everyone in the wider world is at risk. If--that one my mother warned about succeeding then--

Emelyse won't allow herself to complete this thought. "I know it will happen," she voices aloud, like the ominous danger in the distance might understand the words. Every step she takes her closer to it, and Emelyse is uncertain what causes this new unsettling feeling that now rises in her mind, but she's certain it has something to do with *that* building.

Emelyse stops again when she hears the wolf song once more. Now the sound is definitely more ominous, like it warns someone. She frowns and wonders if that *someone* being warned about is *here*. She looks around in all directions. This time she can't determine the direction it comes from. She glances at the massive building on the horizon.

Perhaps, if I can reach that building in the next day or two, I can stay inside it until the wolf wants to go away.

Emelyse doesn't know the danger she faces right now, and that just two days' ride south of here are three men gathered around a small campfire who now study their wolves' behaviour. She doesn't know until days *later* that one of those men is that same one she'd been having awakenings about.

But soon she'll meet another of his kind who'd explored the high mountains when one of his masters told him it will become one of the most important days of his lifetime.

Emelyse walks on, hesitantly at first, but as the oppressing fear in her heart about who she senses to the south grows, she quickens her pace until finally, she's running. She looks up at the building. It seems to grow in size the closer she gets to it, and not just because she's getting closer. The feeling that it somehow played a crucial role in the region grows too.

It was the first place to fall when the northern invaders came, it's where they also were defeated, it's where the future got decided--

Emelyse skids to a halt. *How do I know all that? I'm a Caller. I can't know the past--*She looks around again, in case her assessment is caused only by being so panicked by the wolf song she hears.

The wolf song? Can it trigger knowledge? I read about wolves in the books in the old Temple--

Emelyse isn't certain, and there isn't anyone she can ask either. *Damn you, Mam, you left me less prepared than I should have been--*

Emelyse feels regret soar through her mind. She loves her mother, but at this moment she can't feel that way. Her pace quickens again when she hears more wolf song, but this time it sounds so much closer and for a reason a lot more ominous…

CHAPTER SEVEN

Emelyse pauses at the doorway of the massive building. Or at least she thinks it's a doorway. She glances up first, and she realises the building reminds her of the old Temple of Damrachia in so many ways.

I wonder how old this building is--?

She can't know. She neither has the skill nor any source to tell her. She listens for a moment for the earlier sound that echoed through the landscape, but now her surroundings are eerily still. Emelyse sees darkness ahead and decides against going there, then slowly walks up the stairway. Emelyse looks around and runs her hand across the edge of the image she passes by.

Now that she's indoors, Emelyse realises how tired she feels. She looks for somewhere she can sit down, take her haversack off her back and rest for a time. Perhaps also have a bit of time to remember her life before...

She sits down and places her haversack on the floor. She glances around, again getting a feeling that she's in a place where something will happen in the future, but also getting a feeling that it was a place where something happened in a distant past. She sees black soot on the walls and a gaping hole in the wall through which the wind howls.

Maybe this is where the battle with the northern invaders became decisive.

Emelyse pulls a warm scarf from her haversack and wraps it around herself. She checks in her haversack for what she has left to eat next. It isn't much.

I guess I must find food in the wilderness soon--

She frowns.

Dargu had taught her skills she needs now. He'd taught her to use weapons; something that's unusual among females in Damrachia. A sling in a side pocket of the haversack is still untested for use, and when Emelyse thinks over what she may have to do with it, she concludes that the idea of killing an animal doesn't really appeal to her. The baby vole comes to her mind once again when she thinks about animals she'd need to kill to feed herself in the months of a journey ahead.

I can't do it. I cannot kill an animal. Sorry, Dargu, I'd rather eat berries for all the rest of this journey instead.

Emelyse unwraps the pouch containing the last of her meat. As sits chewing it, her attention turns to the room she's in. She notices its size now. She notices that the departure of those who used it before isn't peaceful.

I wonder what happened here--

There are pieces of parchment and old books on the surrounding floor. Emelyse gets up and picks one of them up from the floor. It's in an unfamiliar dialect, so she puts it back down, and returns to where she'd been sitting when she senses something in her own mind that should have given her a forewarning. But she ignored it…

She sits down rather abruptly. She sits down in that way to avoid her mind's attempt to start an awakening.

No, this isn't happening to me. Not now. I want to be normal. Stop this--

It's useless to try. She knows this. But somehow Emelyse stops the awakening from happening. It's replaced with a flood of memories about her childhood.

Her earliest memory is from when she's just six years old, now over fourteen years ago, almost fifteen years if she'd really thought about it. She is in her old sleeping room, and her mother is there too. She had awoken from a dream of some sort, but now the dream is unknown…

Dargu had arrived a few hours later with a small girl in his arms-- Emelyse suddenly realises her memories had shifted themselves to a later time. She's several years older, and the small girl she sees is no other than Errysa, her lifelong friend.

I miss her so much.

She wonders again why Errysa could not travel with her.

She's too young.

Emelyse knows the answer, but it doesn't stop the overwhelming anger she feels now.

Why do things have to be the way they are? She doesn't know any answers to that question. *Things will change--*

It's that same thought as before. Somehow she knows this to be certain, but *how* or *why* evades her mind once again. *There can't be anyone who is like the northern invaders, or the world won't change ever--*

Her mind is racing now.

"Why would I of all people start to think about someone unknown to me who is supposed to be like the northern invaders?" Emelyse mumbles aloud.

The echo of her voice just mocks her without ever offering an answer to the question she'd asked.

But I heard wolf song. Maybe they're like the northern invaders.

Emelyse doesn't know how close to the truth she *is* regarding those *whose* wolves made the wolf song, or she might have attempted to travel further despite the darkness outside that has settled itself over the land. One part of her questions won't be answered until many years later, and then only by the unknown girl, she has seen in her awakenings.

Emelyse feels so exhausted suddenly and now is having trouble to keep the awakening from her mind. She slumps back against the large carved stone and closes her eyes. The darkness is immediate…

She hears laughter. A man's voice that speaks a dialect she doesn't understand, can be heard now, and then more laughter. A baby cries, but it's in the background. Now also a woman speaks, and this time there's an urgency to the voices which Emelyse cannot shake from her own mind.

Why is the man so insistent that he'll be alright? Hang on, how do I know he said that?

The conflicting thought about the man she hears pulls Emelyse from the awakening she just did. For several moments Emelyse sits dazed, and she wonders where she is. Then suddenly she remembers that she's on her way to a place where she can do her awakening visions in safety. Where no one can harm her or put her in danger…

Emelyse sighs and thinks about whether she should try another awakening. But then a sound alerts her and now her mind races…

Who is out there?

CHAPTER EIGHT

Emelyse holds her breath when she hears a distinct grunt…

A wolf? Here…!

She listens for other wolves but hears none. But then she hears a sound which makes her draw in her breath, and she holds her hands over her mouth. A voice of a man…

"*Kiato*, find who hides here."

He knows I'm here, Emelyse feels panic rise now. She'd heard the *many* retellings about people riding on wolves, who'd apparently taken hold of most of Keldarra. One of them is here *now,* and he's looking for her, it seems.

Emelyse pushes further into the darkness of her hiding place as far as she can go. She feels a stone piercing into her back. She closes her eyes, trying to remain calm. The blackness of an awakening is the last thing she wants.

Not now… not now…

Darkness overwhelms Emelyse's mind once more, just as what happened to her a season earlier when she'd just left Damrachia.

Emelyse screams when in this *unwanted* Awakening she sees a menacing man strike another. The man slumps on the ground, and from what she sees, it's apparent immediately that the man isn't capable of rising. Not unaided, at least. Then she sees a pool of blood form…

Emelyse feels an overwhelming terror rise in her mind. Future is unpredictable, but something about this future seems set like it will happen no matter which way she'd try to alter it. Not even a

Preserver, or even a room full of them, could alter *this* outcome. The event Emelyse that sees in her mind will stay with her until many years later a woman will sit opposite of her in the room and remind her of the terror with her own similar retelling.

Then a darkness overtakes her mind, and she screams again, this time louder, and with a voice that cannot hide the terror she feels. Then silence…

Emelyse feels something cool on her face. She screams again then feels two powerful hands holding her arms, and in her thrashing she hits something--or someone…

"Calm yourself."

A man's voice. Who's here with me?

"I'll let go if you stop swinging your arms around."

Slowly, Emelyse's mind understands what has happened. They warned her about doing too many awakenings in quick succession, while still so untrained and young, and they warned her to *not* do them until she received more training from Jarryca…

Jarryca. Did she send someone here for me?

"No. Let me go--Let me go--" Emelyse screams suddenly.

"Alright, I'll do that, and I'll back away slowly."

"Did Jarryca send you here?" Emelyse calls out.

"Who's that?"

"Who are *you*?" Emelyse demands to know.

Jymar had been travelling past the watchtower, when he'd heard Emelyse's first scream, and had gone to investigate it. He'd found the woman in a slumped heap on the floor. He'd lifted her, then tried to wake her.

"My name is Jymar," he answers to her apparent demand while thinking, *She's beautiful. Maybe too beautiful for her own good--*

He looks her over. She has rich reddish-brown hair, but in the half-dark, he cannot make out the colour of her eyes. He looks at Emelyse, smirking. *Perhaps she'll let me just do it to her--*

Deep down the idea disgusts Jymar. He isn't like most others in City of Wolves who'd go after whatever woman crossing his path in unfortunate circumstances, or by design if such man sought such a woman. Until now he'd not been in that way, but now he has a woman here and a delirious one *too*.

Maybe I can knock her out. Pretend she started thrashing about again, and when she's out, I'll take her--

Emelyse looks at the man. She feels her suspicions grow when his facial expression changes from showing concern to something else.

What does he want from me? Emelyse looks down. She's now feeling uncertain. *Am I feeling this way because of what happened to me? What exactly happened to me?*

She clasps her hands together and waits to see what will happen. There's only silence that answers her questions. And his eyes look her over constantly. She doesn't look to check, but her senses tell her this. Now that the effects of the awakening are getting fewer, Emelyse feels like this encounter with this man isn't by chance. He's after something…

"What *do* you want?" she asks.

"Who, me?" he answers. But he doesn't tell her what he wants.

"What's your name?" she now asks. Her voice is now angry. She looks up and stares at the man with seething eyes filled with an icy hatred for him. *I know what he wants, but he needs to tell me for himself--*

"Are you hungry?" he asks, obviously to evade to the questions the woman opposite of him is hurling at him.

I'm hungry.

She's puzzled for a moment *why*, then glances past the man and sees her haversack lying on its side. Beside it lies a part-eaten piece of meat. She frowns. It's obvious that the man notices her looking behind him, and he turns, and when he looks back at her, he grins broadly.

"You can't eat *that* meat. It looks like it's about to break out in rot."

Emelyse's mouth opens wide in protest, when the wolf lopes to *her* meat-based meal, picks it up and rushes off outside with it.

How did the wolf do that? A wolf? His wolf was here all this time?

"How…?" she asks simply.

Emelyse stares hard at the man, but it just causes him to laugh at *her*--and in that annoying loud way that's making her even angrier.

"Alright, I guess I can explain--" he says, but when he doesn't complete the sentence, Emelyse feels her anger explode.

"Why *are* you here?" she screams.

She only gets a gleeful smile back.

She angers so easily. I wonder how far I can push her, Jymar knows deep down that he doesn't want to be this way. *If Belduran is right I have to be different. But he said she'd be here. How did he know that? How did he know that I'd needed to help her? How did he know she was going to be in trouble in the way I found her…?*

CHAPTER NINE

"Are you *ever* going to answer my questions?" Emelyse snaps at the man.

"My name is Jymar. Someone told me I'd find you here," he mutters the words almost hesitantly.

"Someone told--" Emelyse says, but then stares ahead with a perplexed look on her face.

Mam said no one ever uses this road these days, but he was riding by. He knew I was here--

"How?"

"*Someone* told me to come here--" Jymar replies.

Emelyse frowns again, then she feels puzzled as well. *How would anyone know I came here? Mam said that only she and Dargu knew I was going this way--?*

Emelyse looks at Jymar again and considers a new tact on how she could deal with the situation. But before she can ask anything, Jymar gets up, whistles once, and Emelyse almost jumps up when the dark wolf re-appears in the room.

"I'm going to find a beast to kill for food. Fresh meat *will* give you the strength for travel here," Jymar adds a moment later, "Do *not* leave. The *wolf* will find you fast--"

Emelyse nods once, then she looks down and bites her lip. She still feels weak from the awakening, but she isn't about to tell this to the man. But it's obvious that he can see she's weak, and that his words are just a warning to her that going anywhere in this place at this time of the day would be unsafe for her. She knows he's right.

"I won't go anywhere--" she says in a loud voice just before Jymar disappears through the opening in the wall.

Emelyse hears a few noises, and a few moments after that the distinct sound of an animal running off. She looks at the opening and expects Jymar to come back inside, but he doesn't. She listens and hears only the wind rustling through the trees outside. She is alone again.

I hope he comes back.

Emelyse isn't sure *why* she wants the man *back*. Especially *not* after the way he'd looked at her earlier.

Like he wanted something from me--

There are rumours she'd heard in Damrachia about the western lands; the suggestion about the regions beyond the immediate region around Damrachia is that men will rape and even kill women!

I guess that's why Mam said to me I needed to keep my awakenings under control, and why she'd said that I can't be seen. But who is he? He has a wolf. Was this the wolf I heard in the distance? The sound was too far away for him to have travelled to here too soon.

Emelyse gets up and walks to her haversack, picks it up and returns to the stone she'd been sitting on. She places the haversack somewhat behind her, so she has it in *her* reach: then *the man will need to get past her to reach for it.* Though Emelyse is uncertain, she's able to prevent him from picking it up with his extra body strength.

She closes her eyes for a few moments, and she tries to fight off the feeling of fear that's now invading her mind. She also feels that another awakening wants to assert itself. She breathes in and out slowly, attempting to use the technique her mother had instructed her in the last several years, ever since the First Awakening happened.

That first time when a girl gets a dream is an Awakening.

Emelyse is so certain for a moment she can hear her mother's voice whisper in her mind, that she opens her eyes, and sees Jymar standing in front of her. When he sees that her eyes are open, he grins at her before he speaks, "I hope you like a roasted ailep hound--"

Emelyse frowns again.

When did he get back here? I didn't hear him come at all.

She glances around and now sees the wolf lying down near her with his attention completely focused on her. When the wolf notices she's watching him, he tilts his head in a way that makes Emelyse grin, because it's almost like he says with it, *"What are you looking at?"*

Emelyse stares at the wolf, and just as she focuses on something else, Jymar speaks, "His name is Kiato…"
"The wolf?" Emelyse looks up at the man.
He nods.
She looks at the wolf again.

Something is familiar with the beast. Something is familiar with everything that's happening here now. "You said something about someone telling *you* I was going to be here," Emelyse says, "*Who* told you about…?"

"A person I know told me. Who he's none of your concern," Jymar's answer is abrupt. Emelyse glares at Jymar for a moment because she didn't expect the harsh tone he'd used.

I guess he doesn't want to tell me much about himself.

"Are you hungry?" Jymar asks, obviously changing the subject to suit his own needs.
"I hope *you* don't expect me to cook *that--*" Emelyse spits at him, pointing at the carcass lying on the top of a stone slab.
"Of course not. I'm going to cook," Jymar says, then laughs loud seeing Emelyse's shocked face. "I know how to cook--I've done it for the last seven years of my life--"

If he's as old as I am, that means he started doing that, when he was only thirteen or fourteen years old. He wasn't even at First Rites then--

"What are you sulking about now?" Jymar asks.
"I'm not sulking--I'm thinking--"
"Thinking about what?"

"About why *you* could be here. Mother said--" she begins to say, then stops speaking. *Should I tell him what Mam told me...?*

"I thought you were *alone* here. Where's your mother...?" Jymar's voice now betrays some insecurity on his part. Emelyse notices it immediately.

"My mother is at home--I hope at least she is--" Emelyse says hesitantly, then adds, "and how *do* you know my dialect. You don't speak it like you were born to speak it--"

"You *hope* she is?"

"Yes, I hope she's alright *actually*--" Emelyse spits back at him, now getting angry again.

"I haven't known either of my parents since I was almost thirteen years old," Jymar hisses.

Emelyse notices the pain in the man's voice, almost like he's straining under the weight of emotions he possibly hides every day.

CHAPTER TEN

Emelyse sits staring at the campfire, feeling pensive. She's uncertain what to make of words that Jymar said before he'd stomped off to where the carcass of the dead animal lies, which she sees him carry outside. Then after a few minutes, Jymar is back with the carcass minus head and legs and throws it into the campfire in front of her. Emelyse almost gags for a moment at seeing the dismembered carcass, then looking up, catches a momentary smirk on the man's face.

I'll force myself to eat that, or he'll go on endlessly about how I just acted.

It isn't the first time Emelyse had seen a dead animal because Dargu had often slaughtered their own meals to make sure they never saw her in the city.

"I guess you have seen nothing slaughtered before?" Jymar grins broadly as he asks the question.

"I actually have--But I still find it disgusting--"

Jymar laughs loud. "I guess you lived a life of nutritious food and good clothing where you came from. And where is that exactly?"

Emelyse keeps quiet.

"I *know* I recognise your dialect as one that's spoken by some people where I live--"
"And where *do* you live?"
"Not anywhere where a pretty one like *you* would want to go--" Jymar answers.
"I guess not if they're all as rude as you--" Emelyse spits at the man, remembering his earlier leering at her.
"I'm not rude--" Jymar says, but shrugs his shoulders and turns to check the meat cooking on the campfire.

"You *are--*"

"How?"

"Because in all this time you've been here, you haven't bothered to give me water to drink, or to let me pass water, and you keep looking at me in *that* way--"

Emelyse cries suddenly.

Jymar stands for a moment before he sits down close to the woman. "What's the matter?" He now feels concern and a few other conflicting feelings, which he tries to hide from his voice.

"I miss my home. I miss my mother--" Emelyse sobs loudly now.

"Where is home?"

Emelyse looks at the man and considers whether to say anything. While she considers his question, Jymar realises something as well.

"She'll be from the east, but let her do what she needs to do."

Those were Belduran's words to me before he'd suggested that much of the things going on in recent days would be all by design and not chance. Even said that a man was coming to the city whose presence there will prove how right he is--

"I keep seeing an image in my mind... It's the image of an unknown city. I never know what to make of it... It has many men in it, all with wolves--"

The comment jerks Jymar's attention back to the woman. "How did you see that? Have you been there?"

The words he hears coming from the woman remind Jymar of how *both* Belduran and Rudrig made him aware of the apparent destiny *he* has. They *too* saw things in their minds...

"You'll meet a woman there, and she has important things to tell you. You have two choices. Either you behave like all others here and forgo the destiny we see for you, or you listen to her and you'll shape yourself into the man who has a crucial role in the fulfilment of the future we see. Others will come with their own role to play. But eventually, we all must listen to the prophecy that The Truth really is--"

Jymar feels a nudge in his ribs. He looks angrily in the direction from where it came. He sees a moment of fear in the eyes of the woman next to him. She'd obviously moved nearer to him when she said something to him, and he hadn't answer. He turns bright red when he realises he raised his arm in readiness to strike. Jymar wills himself to lower it slowly.

No, I'm not like the others who want to strike a woman so readily. It's wrong to do that--

Jymar looks away, and his heart fills with a deep shame. He turns back when Emelyse places a hand gently on his arm. He looks at her. She sees his eyes glazed with the tears he is fighting off. He feels her hand to wipe below his right eye. He feels an overwhelming attraction grow for this mysterious woman. He leans forward, intending to kiss her lips.

But then, as sudden as her motion is to soothe his pain by wiping a tear away, she's gone from his side. He stares at Emelyse, who now sits ten paces from him at the southern side of the room. She glares at him angrily. She doesn't want her actions to result in him assuming to do whatever it is he seemed to plan now.

Jymar feels like has has rejected him, and an anger grows inside him. *How dare she reject him?*

He gets up, and he ignores everything that the three Elder Men had said to him about this encounter.

I'm a Wolf Rider, Master Scout, Wolf Master and a man. She should obey my will--

He sees the fear return in the woman's eyes when he walks towards her. She gets up and rushes to the other end of the room intending to leave through its exit and hide somewhere in the building's darkness. A wolf, ordered to stand in her way, blocks her exit. She tries to go towards the opening in the wall, but the wolf again is faster. She backs away when the beast growls in the most menacing way she's ever heard a wild beast growl…

Emelyse stares towards Jymar. He's slowly advancing--almost in slow motion--and to her, the lack of speed makes his actions more menacing than if he'd charged at her. With a wolf to one side and the man on the other side, she realises that her means of escape is diminishing fast, and fears what the man may do to her when he reaches her.

It only takes a few more steps before he reaches her, and Emelyse realises she's pinned against the wall, and feels his lips kissing her face, but because she's moving her head in every direction, he cannot reach her lips…

"No, you don't want this…" she pleads.

CHAPTER ELEVEN

"I don't think you want to do *this* to me--" Emelyse screams in Jymar's face when her plea remains unanswered. Jymar presses closer and scowls at her for rebuking his advances.

"Why not?"

"Because that's *not* your destiny. Your destiny is to be an honourable man, who saves this world," Emelyse screams, "I saw it in this vision I did. I'm a Caller, you know. We can see what future has in store for us, and in the vision I did, when you found me, I saw you standing next to a soldier, and you called him War Ender--"

Jymar stops pushing against the woman and moves somewhat away from her. His face contorts for a moment, then he laughs.

"Me, stand next to some War Ender," he says as he snorts, laughing loudly. "That's nonsense only a scared woman would say and--"

"Doesn't The Truth mention him?" Emelyse spits back at him, "And it's not some War Ender but THE War Ender--"

Jymar stops laughing. How does she know about The Truth?

"How do you know about that?"

"So it's true then--About you."

"What do you mean? The War Ender is a retelling only. He can't exist--"

"They think he exists. Those who sent you here--"

He steps closer again; now for other reasons. The previous

thought about what he wants to do with or to this woman is all but gone from his mind now. It's replaced with a curiosity that he has felt only *once* before. He felt this curiosity when Belduran came to speak with him. The words the old man spoke made him laugh out loud.

"A boy will come here in three years from now, and you'll help me to prepare him for what he'll be doing later--"

"Three years is a long time to wait in a life filled with violence such as *yours--"*

Jymar stares at the woman, tongue-tied now. *How does she know what they said to me?*

"How *do* you--?" he says, but then shuts up. He realises that somehow she already *knows* the answer. She told him, and he'd heard *one* other person mention those words before today: *Belduran!*

"I think the boy is blissfully unaware right now and happily playing with a little girl right now. But in a few years from now, *before* he's ready for his First Rites, he won't be celebrating it with his family, but he'll be fighting against the forces, who wish to cause him and many others harm. There's *one,* who'll arrive in your midst… *never* trust him. He'll rip that boy from his home. I think I'm going to meet him *too,* and the girl he brings, to meet another of her kind--"

Jymar frowns. Emelyse seems to talk about events *now,* which haven't happened yet.

If she's correct in her assessment, they might never happen if--

"What do you *know* of what the future brings?" he spits at her, feeling anger now.

He steps forward again intending to continue his earlier actions and ignores the apparent reality that three different people now have told him about things that are going to happen in years from now.

"No!"

He steps back because he's surprised to hear the force used when she spoke that *one* word. "If you DO what you've on your mind right now, you'll never become the honourable man, you're destined to be.

You won't become the man, who helps the woman mentioned in The Truth. And you'll never help--" Emelyse stops talking, uncertain herself of how much to *tell* the man of his destiny actually.

"Help who?" he asks, with his anger gone now from his voice, and his stance changes. He sits down. "Sit down--I think you convinced me. You and Belduran both have--"

"In what way?"

"In a way that until *now* I was having a hard time accepting or believing--" Jymar answers.

Emelyse stares at him in disbelief. His voice, which first is filled with glee, now sounds gentle, almost sounds like he is talking with a child, and not a woman, who's a few months past Second Rites. To Emelyse realises this man called *Jymar* can't be much older than she is herself.

It seems to Emelyse now that all the previous mannerisms she'd observed in Jymar before, and even moments before, have all but evaporated now. She looks at him, first feeling hesitant, but then realises finally that he'd indeed spoken in a gentle way--not a gentleness with some pretence in it--but with a gentle voice that a man, such as Dargu, would have used when speaking to his daughter Errysa and to Emelyse.

Jymar walks back to the stone block next to where a dying campfire is located. He throws a few pieces of wood on it. Then he looks up and waits to see what Emelyse will do. She walks slowly to her former seating place, and after a few moments standing next to it to see if the man stayed seated, Emelyse sits down too.

"I think I *didn't* want to believe--" Jymar continues, "I thought it was all just a retelling told to entertain us in the city--"

Emelyse decides not to ask about the city he talks about and decides to listen, "And?"

"I don't know anymore--" he replies, then sighs.

There's something else I'm supposed to tell her, but I'm not certain if she'll listen to it after the way I behaved towards her. Damn you, Belduran, for making this so damned hard for me--

"It doesn't matter--I think that it's important that *you* don't tell about *me*--And maybe you *need* to leave soon. It can be hard enough to travel through this area, so I'm going to ride you to about halfway there--I guess you're heading towards Azaquina--"

It's now Emelyse's turn to feel surprised, "How do you...?" she says.

"Belduran told me where the woman I'd meet, is going--"

"Oh, right--If you say he has a skill like mine, then he *would* know that, though I know of *no* man capable of doing visions, *or* having this skill, so maybe he's just guessing--"

"He knows things about my family that I've told no one since arriving--" Jymar blurts out, "And *he* says the boy comes from the *same* city where I was from, and I've never told *that* to anyone either. I wasn't in that city when they snatched me, I was in one called Ruh'nar where it happens more--"

CHAPTER TWELVE

"Ruh'nar? Are you certain you were *there?*" Jymar looks up at the woman sharply, when he notices the venomous tone in which she says the city's name.

"What's wrong about saying its name?" There is an obvious curiosity in Jymar's voice.

"It's where--" she says, but stops.

Can I tell this man about Damrachia?

"Where I lived, they see *that* name as a bad omen--" she says finally.

"A bad omen? In what way?" he leans forward now.

"Something happened a long time ago that caused much hurt, and--" she stops again feeling emotions well up, "It's the cause for *why* I had to leave my home--"

"Oh, right? I guess I somewhat understand your pain. I lost my parents eight, or was it nine, years ago--"

"How?"

"When the Wolf Riders came to Ruh'nar, and I was unfortunate to have been walking in the street," Jymar explains, "and they had snatched me when--"

"Alright, so if you come from the west, and you were visiting there, then how *do* you know my dialect?"

"Rudrig speaks it fluently. He taught it a few of us--"

"So, you learn stuff besides riding a wolf?" Emelyse chuckles somewhat.

"Yes--we *do*," Jymar says defensively.

"Like *what*...?"

Jymar looks up because it almost sounds like she's just enquiring about something interesting rather than something that had the potential of causing her harm.

"I can use that weapon extremely well," Jymar says as he points at his spear arrow thrower. "Vaymaz says I'm among the best--"

"*Who?*"

Jymar now frowns because Emelyse asks like she needs a confirmation for something.

"Vaymaz and why are--?" he asks.

"Because I heard *that* name said in a vision--" Emelyse interjects, interrupting Jymar's explanation.

"So, what do *you* know about him, if like you say, you know stuff about the future?"

"I saw something--I'm uncertain what it is. But it's important, and it'll be something you may need to warn *him* about--" Emelyse says softly, feeling bothered again about the content of the awakening she saw.

"I don't know he'd listen to me."
"I think he *will*. He'll probably tell you it's meant to happen."
"Meant to happen?" Jymar now sounds sceptical.
"Yes," Emelyse answers.
"Tell me what's going to happen--" Jymar whispers.
"I can *show* you what will happen."
"Show me--*how*?" Jymar shrieks out.
"I said I'm a Caller," Emelyse says, "It's our skill to see future events, although this one is one I'm not certain I want to see again--"

Jymar frowns as he thinks, *It seems she's telling me something.*

Something about one person in particular in City of Wolves, whose existence will be crucial, and now from what I can figure out, she's suggesting that something may happen to him.

He's now not certain if he should tell her the message given to him to relay to her…

"How does it work?"

"I'm not yet proficient enough to be very good at it, but I can try at least--" she replies.

"Show me if you can--"

"I guess I won't be the first *or* the last to break these rules. I think the rules for this skill, is what prevents the *truth* to be known," Emelyse mumbles.

Jymar decides not to ask her to explain the words. He'd heard the three Elder Men, who sent him to this watchtower, say similar.

"I need a comfortable place, where I cannot injure myself if I fall over--" Emelyse says in a loud, clear voice.

"You will not like my *best* suggestion then--" Jymar softly chuckles.

"And that is…?" she asks.

He answers her question with a stretched out an arm towards the wolf. She gazes in the direction the man points and swallows hard, realising what he suggests.

"The wolf *can* tell by your body movements whether you'd be alright, and he'd be able to *catch* you if you get what I mean by that--"

She nods.

They both get up, and by some unknown method the man forces the wolf to get up, and he makes the beast pace to a shaded place next to the wall. Here Kiato lies down against the wall with legs splayed out.

She looks at the wolf, then at Jymar, and back at the wolf. "You can lean against his chest. He won't harm you. I gave him a signal to treat you as my equal--"

She nods again, but swallows hard to quell the knot of fear she feels. Emelyse remembers the earlier encounter with the beast *still*. She moves to the animal slowly.

"I think *one* message from Belduran, is going to help you *later*. He says you're meeting *another* with a wolf *later*. He told me to say to you, 'If you overcome your fear of wolves *now*, the wolf that comes with the girl on top, will be one you can accept into your house,' and I don't know what he meant by it because he didn't explain it--"

"I think I know what it means. I can't explain *why*, but I know the meaning of the words," Emelyse says softly, and she's surprised because *now* she sounds self-assured and certain of her own action.

I know the girl he was told about. I don't know her name, but I know that one day I'm going to be meeting her. I need to be brave now as he states--

Emelyse lowers herself down on the dusty floor, looking directly at the wolf who seems to be as inquisitive of her as he'd been the first day.

She smiles. "Will he like it if I stroke him?" she asks, then she looks up at Jymar, who kneels down next to her.

"Lift your hand slowly with the back of it up."

Emelyse nods and looks at the wolf again and lifts her right hand up slowly. Kiato sniffs her hand, then Emelyse has to suppress her giggle, when the wolf's long, raspy and soaked tongue licks over the back of her hand.

"Now lift your hand to his nose bridge and gently place it there but don't move your hand," Jymar says softly, almost in her ear as he'd moved closer to her. She feels a moment of annoyance, thinking he's using this to do *again* what he attempted to do earlier. But when she glances at him, she gets an encouraging nod from him instead.

Emelyse moves her hand on the wolf's nose bridge and then feels the stream of hot air coming from his nostrils down into her sleeve.

Next, Jymar's hand is covering her hand and lifts her hand to the top of the wolf's head. He holds her hand there for several minutes before taking it away…

51

CHAPTER THIRTEEN

Parting is hard for Jymar and Emelyse after the recent events. First, the awakening had shown him how *true* the words were when Belduran and Rudrig spoke to him. The two of them spoke at length about what the future might have in store for them. "I don't think it'll help you if you arrive with me in tow."

Jymar helps Emelyse lift herself from the back of the wolf by holding her arm.

"Beyond this watchtower, the mountains will become lusher and greener, especially in this part of the year."

"I'm grateful you stayed to help me get this far," Emelyse replies. "I know you're right. I think I'll carry this secret to my grave. I think the journey in total would have taken me a *lot* longer. More like three or four years."

"From here--on foot--it will be about four or five months. I'd bring you closer, but the townsfolk would likely see me--and then--"

"I understand. Even with five months the two years in total it took, is much better than the time my mother claims it takes to travel here."

Jymar looks at her a moment, noting some sadness in her voice once more. "Has your mother travelled to here?"

"Not she--but a woman came from *here* to seek her out--at least if I remember correctly, she came to seek a friend my mother had. Someone by the name of Anora who had a daughter too who travelled to *elsewhere*. When it happened, I wasn't even born yet. I think it might have occurred maybe ten or twenty years before I was born--"

"You never told me how old you are."

"I'm now a year past Second Rites."

"Same as I then--Though Second Rites for *you* was undoubtedly different from what it was like for *me*. For me, it means I got to name this wolf Kiato."

"My Second Rites was hurried as I needed to leave *fast*. In the city I lived in, they aren't kind to people of my kind."

Jymar decides *not* to ask her for more details of the city, but the combination of what she'd told him *before* about the city, plus this comment, makes him think again about an earlier thought that passed through his mind.

They say that in North City there's a place where they do things like she can do, but that those there are corrupt or something like that. I wonder it's that from which she is fleeing. If only the Wolf Riders could get inside the city--

"I think you need to go. If you follow this road for a half day or so, you'll find a small cave in which you can find shelter."

Before Emelyse can say anything in response, he turns his wolf and in minutes is a small dot on the horizon before that *too* is gone.

Emelyse watches for a while in the direction the man rode off, but she's certain she's alone again after a few minutes. She turns and walks, after strapping the haversack tighter to her body. She looks at the landscape ahead. She knows where to go because Jymar told her. She wonders for a moment if she'll ever see him again and decides that this will not be the case.

She sets off at a steady pace; a pace that's not too fast and not too slow. Emelyse wonders how far she is from Azaquina. From the information given to her by Jymar. Not that far.

Maybe a just a few more weeks' travel--

"And then what?" Emelyse mumbles before she thinks, *I guess I need somewhere to stay, or at least find that place Mam told me about. I wonder what Jarryca really is like--*

She doesn't know what's next. All she knows that some 'unknown woman' is supposed to live this 'unknown city'--who knows what to do next--and who'll take her in.

Mam said she leads the Temple here. But if the awakenings I've been doing are something to judge the world by, I may find a distinct reality here. She may even be dead by now--

"I wonder *where* this woman Jarryca lives," Emelyse says loudly. "Mam, why were you never clearer with your instructions…?"

Emelyse realises that Jymar is right. The landscape *here* looks easier to traverse, and the air is milder. After a time, Emelyse even binds her coat around her waist, when she realises the air is also warmer here.

The air is milder here, not like home. I have to stop thinking about home. It's not home anymore. Like Jymar said, 'no one' should know where I came from, and also I should remember 'not' to tell about him either. I should make up some retelling about where I come from. If Jymar is right, I need to learn the local dialect as soon as possible and hide my identity from everyone--

"I know Jymar *is* right. And Mam, *too.* They can *never* know where I was from," Emelyse says softly, "And if I *have* that son I saw in my awakenings, I'll hide it even from him. And that girl--I'm uncertain if I can tell her-but as Mam says--most of history right now, is unwritten, and because there are *none* left who can bind events of from the past with the unfolding future that mother sees. I need to practise the words Jymar taught me--"

She stops walking and looks around, realising she must now be near the cave Jymar has pointed out in his descriptions. Emelyse searches her mind, and when she glances around, she sees the outcrop the man described to her. *It looks like he described. I wonder if he uses it often.*

Emelyse climbs the small slope to the cave entrance, then after a moment of hesitation she enters it. Immediate the wind stills and the cave feels warm compared to outside.

"Maybe it has a hidden spring in it somewhere," Emelyse mumbles, "I should stay a day and recover from that long ride on the wolf. I wonder if I ever meet another wolf--"

If her awakening is correct, then she'd meet another of her kind *on* a wolf. Her vision of the future showed a girl with golden brown hair sitting on a large white and grey wolf. Emelyse didn't mention this vision to Jymar, nor did she tell him that the visions had increased as she got closer to Azaquina.

Her destiny in the city definitely is linked with that of an unknown girl whom she'd meet one day…

CHAPTER FOURTEEN

Emelyse wakes up rather late in the day the following day. She's uncertain, but she knows that during the night she had a dream.

"When he's chased, you need to stop."

"I wonder if I'm supposed to tell that to Jymar," Emelyse mumbles, "I'm certain I saw myself speaking with Jymar saying those words, but as I didn't do it when he and I were together, it might mean I'm supposed to meet him again. It means destiny is not set yet--"

Emelyse rolls over and looks around the cave. She wonders about its appearance now. Something she didn't notice when she arrived. Someone heightened the cave with carving tools. Emelyse stores this information in her mind, just in case it is something she'd rely later on upon.

It's an hour before sunset before she sets off again, deciding now that the impending darkness will hide her presence in the landscape. A rising feeling of worry makes her think that she shouldn't arrive in the city during the day. The warning from Jymar makes her also think she should live in the city for a while *before* people notice she's there. Then if they ask, she can just mention she'd travelled there a few years earlier; if she can keep this up for another five years, it's around the right time for the time when according to her awakening she'll meet the man with whom she'll have a son...

"Maybe I should travel slowly so I arrive in a year and then claim I've been in the city a year but that no one noticed me--" Emelyse mumbles. She gets up and lifts her haversack onto the smooth stone surface.

I'll repack, then go for a bathing in the small pool I found.

She places the haversack behind the boulder where it will be hidden from view for the time she takes to bathe. After checking outside to make sure she sees no travellers in the landscape, Emelyse quickly goes to the back of the cave. She'd found the narrow opening a few days earlier, and when she'd squeezed through, it had revealed the reason for the warmth.

In the small cave, beyond where she's located, is a small but adequate steam pool. Not large enough to get in, but the right depth so she can be seated on the edge, and have her feet in it without touching the bottom. She decided not to climb in because she wasn't certain how easy it would be to get out.

Emelyse picks up the small bundle of herbs her mother had packed into the haversack, and that she takes herbs from it to use for washing. After using her cup to pour the hot spring water over her body, Emelyse rubs her body with the herbs. The fragrances from the herbs penetrate her nostrils, making her smile with a happy memory of her mother bathing her as a child.

This feels so good.

Emelyse takes her time to wash thoroughly, then dresses in clean clothing. If she needs to go to the town soon, she wants to appear as someone better off, not like someone who might be begging. She sits down to eat something before she would depart. Part of the last piece of roasted ailep hound would do well as a dinner. She pulls a large piece from the haunch, wraps the rest back into the leather wrapping, then walks to a small boulder just outside the cave to sit there to eat. As she sits there, she realises the sun now warms her face and that the wind has settled. She smiles.

This is more like the summer weather of--

"No, I shouldn't be thinking about *that* anymore--" Emelyse says aloud. She wonders what she can tell people if they ask *who* she is, and *where* she's from. Then also there's the problem of finding the woman called Jarryca, and to convince her of who she really is, and *why* she, Emelyse, sought her. She isn't certain of many things, least of all her own awakenings. She'd defended them from the apparent ridicule that Jymar had seemed to express whenever they'd talked. She feels all the time he has things to tell her, but he never had spoken of them. And then there's his sudden departure, which made his motivations suspect.

He's not the man I see in my visions destined to be a father to my son-- Emelyse sighs, suddenly feeling the same way she'd done in the first days after leaving her mother. She should feel glad about almost being at her destination, but *something* holds her back. *Something,* she isn't sure what is causing a new feeling of fear growing inside her.

Emelyse focuses her mind on her friend Errysa.

I miss her. I hope she's safe. I hope she'll be safe. I hope Dargu can send her here when she's older so she can come to live with me--

For a while Emelyse sits staring ahead in a pensive mood, then she gets going. It's already almost the middle of the day, and now she felt like she'd been putting off advance to the city too long. On a clear day, she could see its highest buildings in the distance. But not the building her mother had described to her.

A sound distracts Emelyse from her mind's game of thought. She looks up in the direction where she can hear the sound coming.

I'm not sure, but it almost sounds like wolf song. I thought that Jymar said none came so close to the city--

A moment later Emelyse pales, when she sees a familiar man riding towards the small clearing she called *home* for a half year now.

"I thought you wanted to get to Azaquina--"

Jymar dismounts from Kiato, who accepts a now familiar scratch from Emelyse.

"I'm making sure I know their dialect before I get into the city--" she replies, "I was actually planning to go in a few days."

Jymar looks around and sees her haversack packed, then he speaks, "Before you go, I need to speak to you. They sent here me--"

CHAPTER FIFTEEN

"I haven't been totally honest with you--"

Emelyse looks up at the man sitting opposite of her. The confession isn't entirely surprising to her. She has suspected, since their first encounter years earlier, that Jymar hides things from her. More things, perhaps, than he'd himself wanted to admit to, either now or any time in the future.

"What are you trying to tell me, Jymar?" Emelyse's scepticism is clear in her voice.

"Remember when we first met. I suggested to you I wanted to lie with you--" Jymar looks down, feeling shame for the earlier behaviour.

"I remember--" Emelyse says coldly.

"I don't know why I sought you out here, so close to this city, where I'm the one in danger, but a man at the city I'm from told me to come to find you--"

"What's so different now from three years ago, when you found me at that watchtower?"

"Something he told me. He told me I needed to listen to you, but also to tell you a message."

"Did you tell him about me?" Emelyse asks, "I thought you'd keep it secret from everyone--"

"I did! He--errr--Belduran--walked to me one morning and told me that things are changing. He says a boy arrived recently in the city who's going to change things. He says that you know about a girl who's crucial in this too--"

Emelyse pales when she hears the words spoken, then she blurts out, "When he's chased you need to stop--"

"Huh, what do you mean by that?"

"Don't tell me you forgot what I said three years ago," Emelyse scolds him. She stares hard at him, in a way that looks familiar to him, in a way she'd looked at him when he felt tempted to ignore Belduran's words.

"I remember, and until Belduran spoke to me, I thought you'd said it to rebuke me for what I am."

"I didn't say it for that reason. I said it--because--errr--because I have a gift--" Emelyse stammers somewhat, because she isn't sure how much she should tell, and she's certain that he wouldn't remember her mentioning it previously. Jymar's next words have her going even paler.

"I think Belduran shares your gift because he seems to know things that no one should know, and he's not alone in this--"

They sit staring at the small campfire between them, each in a pensive mood. They catch each in a momentary moment of self-doubt and curiosity in equal measures about how things could be a fluke. Emelyse knows it's in part down to the way she'd altered the mind of the man sitting opposite, only because she didn't want to become the object of his desires. Somehow, with this, she set in motion events that now change that man's life.

"I don't think our meeting originally was by chance either," she states in a soft voice. "I think my mother knew that I'd meet you. She said there were two messages I had to give. The first one, she said, is for a man with a wolf, the second one is for a man who also has a wolf but will come to me with a girl--no not a girl, she'll be almost a woman herself by the time I meet her. He's going to be instrumental to bring the child--a boy--I'm going to have, back to me. She's one of my kind, but not--"

Jymar listens in fascination to the woman sitting opposite of him. Until the conversation with Belduran, he'd been sceptical of the future that man suggested, but now as he listens to Emelyse he wonders.

Can it all be really true? Maybe I need to help Belduran with the boy--

"Emelyse, there's one thing in all this you *need* to remember to do."

"What?"

"Tell no one about meeting *me* where you're going. There could be complications for *you* if you do. I think the city you're going to isn't entirely safe, so if you have that son you mention, make sure he's never alone in the city--just in case they--" Jymar doesn't finish the sentence.

"I understand what you mean, Jymar, but I cannot alter fate. We don't have the people around anymore, who could steer the world differently than what fate wants to give us now. I think fate means to take my son from me--by your kind, but then one of your own will also return him. This is the man that you shouldn't *stop* from doing this, it's that man who you need to stop chasing. If you do that, the person who's with him will start the change, that'll make the world better. She doesn't know it yet, and I think she's only just discovering what her own destiny is--" Jymar sits staring at Emelyse. She stares back at him. "We need to pretend that us meeting one another--now or back then--ever happened. I need to walk from here, and then you can never come to seek me out. But make sure you do the things this man Belduran says and make sure you stop chasing him--"

Emelyse gets up, stares intently at Jymar for a moment, then she walks away.

I'm never coming back to this place I used as a house. I have to find somewhere more suited, safer for me. I have to meet the man who'll give me that son--

She doesn't know how long Jymar sits there thinking. She doesn't know how much she changed him until he returns to that mysterious *city* he'd mentioned several times. When he finally goes, he goes to help to set in motion the changes, that Belduran says, are needed. He goes back to teach that boy she mentioned, to teach him what he needs to know to alter the world.

Neither of them knows *what* Belduran's role in all these events is, and why *he* so inexplicably allowed two strangers to meet one another *twice*.

Emelyse glances behind her to make sure she isn't followed, and after a few minutes she sets off at a fast sprint. She needs to get to the beach where she'd seen a man who looks so very familiar to her…

CHAPTER SIXTEEN

Emelyse sits down on a stone. She looks in each direction along the beach. She's uncertain if she's early or late for the encounter with the man she knows she has to meet *here*. She doesn't know when…

Emelyse develops a routine. She'd spend a day, or sometimes a half day, doing work in the city. She wears a scarf tied around her head while doing it. She even rubs some moss ash on her face to appear to be a beggar looking for day work and does the work in some old clothes she finds in a heap near the southern end of the city. Later she'd wash, dress in her beautiful blue dress, being worn because she'd seen herself wearing this in the awakening, and she wears her hair part-braided and uncovered.

It seems people don't notice me when I'm well dressed, notice me more when I wear the rags--

After about thirty minutes of sitting, Emelyse decides that this day wasn't the day she saw in her awakening either.

Every time she walks back to where her dwelling is, Emelyse feels her heart sink a bit more. And today her heart feels like it won't go on anymore. She knows she's in an unfamiliar place, far from any who'd loved her, and the mysterious woman she sought seems like she has vanished. She cannot even find the Temple her mother had told her about.

Emelyse slumps down, feeling despondent. Three years of trying to figure out *where* the building is located, which her mother had told her about, is taking its toll on her. Her gift of foresight will not help her as it locks away the knowledge in the *past*, and as a Caller, she doesn't have access to *that* skill. She needs the help of a Keeper if she's going to find the building on her own.

Her place that she calls a 'home,' is becoming *too* dangerous as people started asking questions about where she lives. So she leaves it…

She'd wandered the street for days, and finally sits down on the log next to the narrow path on the eastern side of the city where the population of this strange city--whose name she's most curious about--is the sparsest. Azaquina is a name mentioned *once* in a text her mother insisted she had to read. In that text, it's referred to as one of seven ancient cities, and the *first* one to fall to the ancient enemy.

"I've been in the city for a while, and I think I'm lost," Emelyse speaks when she sees the man passing her position. The man stops and looks behind him with evident surprise on his face.

"I'm Jerid."

Jerid appraises the woman, who'd spoken to him for a few moments. She stares directly at him, even though she hides behind a bush--seemingly to keep herself out of view of others in the city.

It's him.

"Who are you? And what can I help you with? I'm uncertain I've ever seen you about--"

"My name is Emelyse," she says hesitantly, "I come from far. I'm looking for a place I was told about. I was--errr--told by someone *not* to tell how long I've travelled, but to be honest I'm tired of travel. I've been searching for the last five years--of which two years have been here in this town--and this *someone* told me to pretend I've only travelled two years--I'm uncertain *why* I'm telling you all this--"

"What place might that be?"

Jerid is now curious about the strange accent of the woman. She speaks *his* dialect, but it's clear she'd learnt it through *other* means than being born with it. "If you *need* to keep a secret, then so be it, but believe me when I tell you I'll keep all yours. You fascinate me. I'll help in any way I can--And I don't know why I'm telling this to a woman I've only just met either--"

Jerid and Emelyse grin at each other for a moment, realising they'd, in fact, met a person who could easily be a life partner. Life partners usually recognise one another in some inexplicable way…

"We know the building as a Temple--" Emelyse sees the man frown for a moment. Emelyse is certain she said the *wrong* thing.

"I think you need to *come* with me to my house," Jerid says with a solemn voice, "I think the place you're looking for doesn't exist anymore. I'll be able to tell *you* what happened, but perhaps I should introduce *you* to someone who can do that *better* than I--"

THE END

65

Bergas

CHAPTER ONE

"Bergas--" A small boy of around ten years in age glances up when he hears his name called out. He grins when he sees a familiar man wave at him, "Are you ready to go fishing with your *father*...?" the man calls out.

Bergas nods.

"Are we going to the cave you mentioned to me, Papa?" he looks up with pleading eyes at the tall man.

"Your mother told me to be *careful* when taking you with me--But it's up to *her* to decide whether you can go."

"Jerid--"

Both the boy and man look to where the voice comes from, and a woman with reddish-brown hair is rushing towards them. She stops next to them, then needs to catch her breath for a moment, which makes it obvious she's been running part way. She holds a package against her chest.

"I made--food--yes, I made--food for *both*--of you," she says between her panting.

"I can go with him, Mam?"

"Yes, Bergas, you can go with him."

"Go put your stuff in the boat, while I say goodbye to your mother."

The boy, Bergas, runs off up a hill, and some ten minutes later is back with a small bag that he stows into a nearby boat before climbing into it himself.

"You *be* careful, Jerid," the woman says softly.

"Emelyse, take that worried grimace from your face. Nothing will happen to either of us," Jerid says, then he lifts the woman's chin and kisses her lips. She accepts the gesture with a radiant smile. She loves this man, even if the way or reasons they fell in love are unusual. He knows it too and vows every day to keep her secrets safe soon after they'd met.

They'd become life partners a year before Bergas is born. And unusual as it is for it to be done so soon--within weeks of the first meeting--they'd committed to the ceremony. Most people in the city were bemused when they saw this happen, as they'd always only known the mysterious woman as some sort of beggar.

When the child arrived a year later, and then soon after Emelyse visits the library of the mysterious Jarryca, some even claim that the old woman had a hand in what happened. At about eighty-six years at the time of Emelyse's first visit, they already consider Jarryca old. Emelyse is curious about the old woman when she's greeted with words in her *own* native dialect and not the dialect spoken in Azaquina. She never answer*s* *how* the woman knows her particular dialect…

Man and woman look at each other for a few minutes, then both look in the direction where their son waits. He smiles knowingly at them when he sees his parents look towards him. They smile back at the boy.

"You'll keep him safe…?"
"I *will*. Don't worry. Nothing will happen."

He turns and also climbs into the boat, then with the help of two men standing on the pier, he pushes off. Bergas waves up to his mother, blissfully unaware of his mother's misgivings as she waves back, smiling at him, and therefore *hoping* she hides her genuine feelings. But her son *is* often as perceptive as she, and Emelyse doesn't notice the momentary frown that appears on the boy's face. Sometimes even a person who in secret reminds herself she is a *Caller*, can be fooled by the behaviour of a boy at an age when he becomes more inquisitive than might be good for him…

Bergas turns in the boat quickly and smiles at his father, who's distracted enough to assume the boy just smiles because he's finally going on a boat trip with him.

"Papa, can I help at the harbour when we return?" Bergas grins broadly and pays more attention to the work going on than to his father's face now looking grim, and who's looking up at the woman standing on the pier now clutching her chest and looking pale.

"I don't think that's safe, son," he answers, after seeing a gentle shaking coming from Emelyse, who'd heard the question, then he adds in a softer, quieter tone, "We'll see--"

Bergas nods, then he looks towards each of his parents to see what may be going on with them. He'd noticed his mother becoming more withdrawn in recent months, like she's scared about something. He tries to keep his face neutral. He always knows, when something worries his parents, and he's possibly is as perceptive as his mother, though his young mind doesn't yet understand that he'd, in fact, inherited a skill that she keeps hidden, and that his father has himself sworn to secrecy about.

Maybe they quarrelled and don't want to tell me about it--

Though Bergas tries to convince himself that this is the situation right now, the embrace shown by his parents' moments earlier says otherwise. But he *knows* something is going on…

The changes had started over three years earlier. When he'd

wanted to play, his mother would tell him to stay home. He'd go out by sneaking out, and when he got home, his parents were *both* extremely angry. Then the attack came…

After the attack, he's never far from his father's side, and his mother won't let him go fishing with his father as she'd once let him do.

I wonder what's different today--

"Help me with this rope," Jerid calls out.
"Alright, Papa," Bergas replies, grinning.

Bergas gets up and walks to the stern of the ship where his father hands him one end of the rope. Between them, they wind it into a tight coil. Jerid nods.

"Sit down while we travel."

Bergas complies then waves at his mother is still watching them. She waves after a moment's hesitation, and it makes Bergas frown once again, wondering why she isn't so enthusiastic.

It's a mystery he vows to solve, yet as his mind races over the potential causes, Bergas doesn't realise that this journey will be one of the *last* he'd make with his father…

CHAPTER TWO

The boat trip takes Jerid and Bergas across the massive Bay of Whispers in a matter of days. Bergas sits on the port side of the boat, watching the landscape glide by. He has a dreamy smile on his face. "Papa, what are those animals, there?" Bergas asks when he sees something swimming alongside the boat.

"Those are blue razorfin sharks on their way to their nesting waters," Jerid says, smiling at the boy; he remembers a similar conversation with his *own* father, with his much older brother Hadukin by his side. "Have I told you ever that your Uncle Hadukin, and I *also* saw these sharks when I was about the *same* age as you are now…?"

Bergas shakes his head.

"I think it's perhaps forty years ago. I was almost eleven years old, like you are right now. Uncle Hadukin is twenty years older than I am, so he was already a grown man," Jerid says quietly. "We were fishing for the last time in the year before it was winter, and that's when I saw the sharks--"

"What do they eat?" Bergas asks, looking over the bulwark of the ship into the ocean that's about five paces below him, where six of the majestic-looking beasts swim slowly alongside the boat. "You've seen the red crustaceans that most fishers use. We got some in the crate at the back of the boat, the aft, if you've not seen it before," Jerid says, pointing at a dark box.

Bergas gets up and walks carefully to the box, and lifts its lid. "Can I feed some to them?" he asks.

"Of course. Their motion in the water as they swim around for the crustaceans will bring the fish we want to catch," Jerid explains, grinning. "Use the scoop on the rope next to it to get it out of the box--"

Bergas picks up the scoop that his father shows and lifts a large quantity of the crustaceans from the box. "Come over here with it, and I'll show you what to do," Jerid says. Bergas complies, then watches his father spread the crustaceans in the water, which takes on the appearance of a torrent caused by a storm.

"Do the same, and by the fifth scoop we'll have fed enough for other fish to come," Jerid explains, "and then we'll be reeling in a feast for the spring celebration next year. The fish will get dried between now and then."

Bergas nods. He always is looking forward to the spring celebration with its endless hours of music, eating and drinking refreshing drinks. He keeps quiet about the disturbing dream he's been having where he'd see himself be grabbed by someone on a wolf just as the celebration starts…

Bergas watches the colour of the water turn a pinkish red, then he sees something snapping at the mixture. The sharks seem to have gone, and now equally large fishes are swimming in their place. He's in awe at the spectacle in the water. Bergas looks up at his father as he also leans on the bulwark to watch the fish have their fill.

"More will come, and those will be the tender young ones, which are the best for the feast," Jerid explains.

"Why do we take the young ones?" Bergas asks.

"As a reminder that there was a period in this land's history when things weren't as they're now. That once someone else dictated when we ate, slept, and when we loved--" Jerid says solemnly. "Mam says that's when the northern invaders were here--" Bergas responds, imitating his father's solemn tone.

His father nods in response.

For a period both father and son are silent, both watching the movement in the water. Then Bergas feels his father's hand over his arm. When he looks up, his father holds his finger over his mouth. He points. When Bergas looks in the direction his father points, he spots smaller fishes swimming sidelong.

"Those are the younger fish," Jerid says. "Be silent as noise will spook them."

Bergas nods and quietly climbs down from the wooden beam he'd been kneeling on for the last hour. He watches as his father quickly prepares a fine-woven net, which he lowers into the water from the bow of the ship.

"The current will spread the net out, and the fish will entangle themselves in it thinking it's seaweed," Jerid explains. "Then we lift this net out of the water and we'll have maybe two or three dozen fishes to share with the townspeople for the feast."

Bergas smiles.

It sounds reasonable for him to share the food with others. The whole idea of the spring celebration is to show that sharing food is a positive action all can benefit from. He and his mother had been preparing the cold room for their share of the fish in the last few weeks.

After they complete their task of hauling in all the fish, Jerid hoists the mainsail and sets their destination towards the caves, where they'll collect the caranimia pearls, which his father trades with the tailors and jewel makers of the city. The shellfish that produce these pearls live in a cave his father is going to visit today. Bergas looks forward to the visit. His father told retellings about the caves for as long as he remembers. He imagines it to be a small cave, but his father always claimed it is larger than any person can measure it. And they'd sail inside with the boat…

The rest of the journey to the cave is uneventful, with Jerid explaining things about how the boat is constructed, pointing out certain fish in the sea, and then telling a wide-eyed Bergas about the Northern Blades which tower so high above them that the tips of the highest mountain peaks hide in clouds. Bergas cranes his neck to look to the top of the mountain which seems to plummet directly into the ocean with no sign of a beach.

Bergas sees occasional pieces of ice sheer off the side of the mountain and plummets into the ocean below, and each time he sees this he looks at his father with fear in his eyes.

"It won't happen near the cave," Jerid says softly. He knows he can't say *anything* to still the fear in the boy's mind. This is a danger of the ocean trek the boy needs to learn by himself…

73

CHAPTER THREE

Bergas gazes in awe as their boat comes nearer to the cave he'd been told about by his father frequently. The cave is larger than his young mind can envisage. "It looks so big," Bergas mutters under his breath.

The sheer surprise in the boy's voice brings a broad smile to Jerid's face, who remembers a similar reaction when his own father brought him here.

"It's even bigger than you can even imagine, but we'd need to have thirty or more lighting up the inside with beacons to get an idea of the vastness of the cave," Jerid explains. "The shellfish live *deep* inside the cave. They shun daylight in this part of the year, and the darkness helps the pearls form on their backs."

"How are we getting the pearls from them?" Bergas asks.

"They designed the crate next to you to get them to *want* to climb inside it. It has a lure inside that attracts them. When there are enough inside, we'll pull it from the water, and using this pronged device we lift them from the top one by one, which is what I'll be doing, and you use the knife in the sheath beside you to scrape the pearls loose into the box here--" Jerid explains. "But don't assume it to be easy. The pearls won't release so easily. We'll be busy for several days or even a week doing this…"

Bergas swallows hard, then nods. He hadn't realised that he'd be required to help. He looks again at cave they're now approaching fast. He sees a few other boats ahead of theirs that are also going inside it.

"They're also here for the pearls. Each of has a designated area inside the cave for our work," Jerid explains when he sees Bergas frown for a moment then the boys asks, "How many *do* we need to get?"

"As many as possible. I don't go here every year, and the *more* we collect, the better it is. If we get enough this year, it means I can *stop* fishing in two years from now. Your mother wants me to stop this because--" Jerid says, but then he stops talking.

Better not make the boy worried--

Jerid turns to check their approach to the cave so he won't show Bergas that a frown has formed itself on his face. His own earlier worry has returned in the last few hours. He sees one of the nearby fishers wave at him so he waves back, then raises both fists up side by side a hand lengths distance between them to show that he's not here alone. It's the recognised method by which fishers make each other aware of the presence of others. The approaching fisher acknowledges the gesture with crossed arms with his fists clenched to understand he understood.

"I can show you the tools you'll be using for this task. My father had me practising on some touch leather to learn how to gouge out the pearls from the shellfish. Their exterior isn't so unlike the leather behind you on the deck--"

Bergas looks behind him for the leather his father described. He picks it up and looks it over, and notices that there are many small notches pockmarking the surface.

I thought the animals scurrying around for food on these boats made these marks--

Father and son stare at one another for several minutes, saying nothing. Each knows in their own way *why* they both ended up on a trip together. It seems in Jerid's mind now that the boy is feeling rather reluctant about being here once he'd realised he has to pull his weight. But Emelyse had told him to make sure that the boy learnt skills on this trip. That the boy learnt to survive, to cope, to become knowledgeable, to mark a place in the new existence he'd find himself in *before* he's old enough for First Rites. How this will happen is something Emelyse can never voice, though Jerid always notes her sadness whenever she deflects his questions...

"Practise your skill on *that* leather," Jerid says more forcefully than he means. The frown on Bergas's face shows he doesn't like what his father just told him, or more precisely *how* he said it, and Jerid's own thoughts betray why, perhaps.

There will be harsher times ahead, so he needs to learn to understand not all speak to him in a friendly voice. There will come a time that Emelyse warns me about, but she swore me to secrecy. Perhaps in my own way, I can warn him of what may happen--

Bergas pulls the leather towards himself, muttering under his breath about how *unfair* it is to ruin *his* fishing adventure with such annoying tasks. Jerid notices how similar his son behaves to how he had behaved the first time he'd gone on this sort of trip with his own father. He smiles briefly at the memory his son evokes for him, but quickly looks serious once more before Bergas might see him smile…

Jerid knows the work of collecting the pearls is hard work for an adult man like himself and knows that perhaps this is one of the last times he could take his son on any trip.

"When we're done here, we'll go up into the mountains above and you'll see the wolves--" Jerid says softly. Bergas glances up. "Wolves? What wolves?" he asks.

"Those living in the Northern Blades. Then I'm going to take you east to Upper Plains. There's--something your mother *wants* you to see there before it's too late--"

Jerid stops talking and looks down.

Too late for what?

Bergas had heard those words several times already, and each time his parents say them they seem to take on a more ominous tone. And then there's the fear he feels more and more about the dreams he'd dream at night, which he doesn't want to tell his parents about. The dream of an ominous city, another of a city filled with menacing wolves, and then the last one of just days earlier of his father's boat drifting on the ocean overturned by some sort of storm.

I cannot tell them of my fears when their own fears are so obvious. And why is Papa showing me wolves? Do they know somehow I dream about them?

"What sort of wolves are they? Are they like the ailep hounds we hunt?" Bergas asks.

"No, these wolves are the same type of wolves as in the legend my father once told me about. When we're home, I will tell you that legend…" is the answer softly spoken from the other end of the boat.

CHAPTER FOUR

"This is where we get the pearls from--" Jerid's voice echoes through the expansive cave structure that he and Bergas had entered not so long ago.

Bergas looks around in the massive cave. The echo shows it is much larger than he can even imagine in his mind. The reach of the tall torch his father holds can only reach so far. The boy decides he has seen none place as massive as this cave is, "How long ago did they find this cave?" he asks.

"It's said that this cave was already in use in the Old Days and long before that--" Jerid answers.

"What are the Old Days?" Bergas asks, looking at his father with an obvious inquisitive look on his face.

"It's during the ancient time, long before the northern invaders flooded this land with their evil deeds. Some say--some say that there are still those who pursue these same deeds, but none know if this is true or not," Jerid continues explaining.

Bergas frowns for a moment. He noted a moment of hesitation in his father's voice.

Maybe these 'some' he speaks of are those who made Mam come from the east to here. They can't know that I've heard them talk about where she's from--

"Where did those northern invaders come from?"

"From a land far from here--" Jerid points into the general direction he'd been told by his own father where this land might be located, "My father told me the retelling of them a long time ago. I'll tell you about them in greater detail when we get home. But now-- Now I'll tell you about Mountain Ghost. That's a lesson your mother says: that you'll teach another person one day. I've no idea what she means by those words, but it's that conversation that will create a friendship that will go as deep as the love between brothers--"

Bergas nods, then he asks, "The wolves you're going to show me. Are they somehow related to the retelling of Mountain Ghost?"

"Yes, son."

Bergas quietly makes notches in the leather, while he thinks about what his father has explained. Suddenly he wants just to be a boy who helps his father with his fishing duties, and not, as his own mind tells him, be someone to whom something terrible can or will happen.

"Papa, why do you think there are people out there who want to invade us?"

The question is met with icy silence.

Bergas looks up at his father, who sits unmoving and shakes his head, but not in response to Bergas asking or because he looks up at his father. The usual banter between father and son is very absent today. It takes a while before his father speaks, and he decides to tell the retelling of the wolf he'd mentioned moments earlier...

"They say that the wolf has retellings depending on whom you talk to," Jerid says in a quiet voice. "The retelling they'll want you to believe is that he's the first of *their* kind. But the real retelling is, that he saved this land from those northern invaders--She and her brave master did. Your mother is certain you'll be told this retelling to another one day--"

It amazes Bergas that his father is so open and frank about something he probably doesn't want to talk about.

But what's going on?

He isn't certain who the *'they'* in his father's words is, but that it somehow involves him is certain from the sadness in his father's voice. He knows his parents shield him from the harshness of life outside their home in the hills, and the few times he has gone into town it's *always* with both his parents. And then there are his recent dreams. Bergas doesn't quite understand them. He sees himself as an older boy in them, but *not* with his parents, and *not* in the familiar surroundings of Azaquina…

Bergas pays attention to his surroundings as they're now entering the deeper parts of the cave. The many lights ahead of them show that many other fishers from the city are here too. He sees dozens of boats of every size; some with one person in it, others with ten occupying the boat. Greetings echo through the massive cave.

Bergas stares around him into the blackness of the cave beyond the torches that are being lit up one by one by the various fishers around their boat, and then he glances at his father doing the same with three torches around their own boat. The increase in luminosity makes him look around again. The glimpses of what Bergas can see leaves him breathless. He looks everywhere.

"There are so many people here--" Bergas mutters under his breath.
"The reason for that, my son, is the number of shellfish that gather here at this time of the year."
"Why are there so many of them?"
"It's their breeding season soon. We're *not* killing them, well not most of them, just those that are the largest that we need for the feast--and we'll harvest the pearls that form on their backs as well," Jerid explains.

"And if we get enough of them, we never must make this trip again?"

"No, *we* won't return after this day. And *you* won't need to do this work either if you help your old father with gathering as many of the pearls as you can manage--"

"I'll do my best, Papa."

Bergas smiles broadly. He got a nod to confirm that he'd given an answer that his father appreciates.
"Are these notches done right?" Bergas now asks, feeling happier now about the task ahead of them.
"Yes, you're fast at learning, it seems. You're doing a better job with it than I did at your age the first time when it was I'd come here with my father--And like *you,* I didn't really like it at all," Jerid says, grinning. His smile broadens even more when his son blushes.

"I think you deserve the trip I got planned for us if you work hard over the next few days--" Jerid says.

"I will, Papa, I *will*--" Bergas replies.

CHAPTER FIVE

Bergas lifts another basket from the wooden platform, when a voice bellows out and echoes through the cave, "Bergas, come to greet your uncle and his two friends--"

Bergas looks up, and he sees a taller man standing beside his father, and a grin of recognition flashes over his face.

"Uncle Hadukin--" he calls out.

Bergas runs towards two arms held apart, then a moment later is in his uncle's arms. Although in reality, Hadukin was actually his father's uncle, the old man didn't mind being treated to the same sentiment from the youngster now embracing him.

"You remember Draigus and Timorin?" Hadukin asks.

Bergas glances at the two companions of his uncle, both just past Second Rites. He nods in recognition.

"I remember you this tall," Timorin says, holding his hand at Bergas's waist.

"I think he was more like this tall--" Draigus adds.

Both of them laugh loud, and after a moment of frowning, Bergas laughs as well.

"But now you're growing into a capable man, and I'm certain that one day you'll stand proudly beside your father as a tall man," Timorin says.

Bergas frowns a moment, and in a sideways glance catches his father frowning too. He quickly looks away so his father doesn't see.

"Are you learning a lot here?" Draigus asks.

Bergas nods.

"Your father and uncle taught me," Draigus says. "I could teach everything I know."

"I would love that--" Bergas replies somewhat hesitantly.

He doesn't want these two men to tease him for things he doesn't like.

"I think I know what interests you *more* than fishing," Draigus says gently. "I think boat building is more your thing--"

Bergas nods vigorously before he can stop himself.

"My father builds boats at the harbour. I'm certain you can start out by learning how to repair them," Draigus continues. "But you'd need to ask your parents *first* to make sure it's alright for you do it."

"Is it hard work?" Bergas asks hesitantly.

"It can be, but you'd be working on the smaller boats with me at first--if your father approves of this plan," Draigus says softly.

Bergas nods. He understands that he had to start out as some sort of apprentice.

"Shall I help you with what you're doing?" Draigus asks. "With both of us doing it, you'll be done faster, and you'll have many more pearls for your father to sell."

Bergas nods then pulls the crate with crustaceans closer to where he'd been sitting, and after a moment Draigus takes over and lifts the heavy crate with one hand and quickly places it at a wider section of the boat, so he and the boy can sit opposite of one another to do their work. Bergas smiles a grateful smile at the man. His arms ache from the work done so far.

"How many of these have you collected so far...?" Draigus asks.

"I got these three bags filled with them. I started early each day. I want *Papa* to *stop--*" Bergas says.

He lets out a sob suddenly. He didn't realise how much the words his father had spoken earlier actually had affected him. He looks down.

Draigus frowns and looks carefully at the boy opposite of him, then gives a sideways glance at the two older men standing on the stern of the ship, talking to one another in hushed tones drowned out by the buzz of the voices of the surrounding fishers. He wonders if something is going on.

Draigus turns his attention back to the task at hand. It isn't his place to interfere in another family's problems. He is aware of the unusual reasons of how Jerid chose this boy's mother as his life partner. He regards the young boy as a friend.

I'll make sure he keeps safe and well when he can convince his parents to let him help me...

"Draigus, can I ask you something?" Bergas asks hesitantly.

"Of course, what do you want to know?" Draigus answers.

Bergas is silent for several minutes, and Draigus notices the sideways glance the boy makes towards where his father talks to Hadukin. Hadukin, who is about two decades older than the boy's father, is a formidable presence. He and his brother Jerid both are tall, broad-shouldered, and although they whisper, the timbre of their voices carries in the massive cave like the buzz of bees. They can impose it to strangers to hear them speak; it's also imposing to a young boy not secure of his emotions. Draigus is certain that the sound makes the boy nervous because one can't ever be sure from it whether they do the conversation in anger or otherwise. The constant frown that Draigus catches on the boy's father's face also doesn't help.

"I want--errr--to know something--" Bergas whispers.

"Is something wrong?" Draigus asks cautiously.

"I think--I think my parents are angry with me--or with one another--" Bergas whispers.

"You know they *love* each other. People find it strange that two people can life partners so soon. And I don't think either is angry with you," Draigus responds, then places a hand on the boy's shoulder. "Tell me why you think that--"

"I think something is going on but they--" Bergas explains, quickly glancing first towards his father to make sure he isn't too near, then continues, "I think they know something that will happen to me. I don't how or why though. I remember going to that old woman in the library in the city with Mam and she--"

"You mean your mother took you to see the crazy old woman…?" Draigus says.

"She isn't crazy--" Bergas responds defensively, glaring at Draigus for a moment.

"Alright, alright--But what has it to do with *you* thinking there's something wrong between your parents?" Draigus asks softly.

Deep down, Draigus knows how the boy feels. His own parents had broken their pledge to be life partners, and he'd moved to another house with his mother, who then later chose another man to be her new life partner. As he grew up, Draigus learnt that this could happen, though not so often.

"I think I'm in trouble. I keep dreaming about men on wolves--" Bergas blurts out.

CHAPTER SIX

"What *do* you mean by 'men on wolves'?" Draigus asks slowly, lowering his voice even more so that there's no chance for the boy's father or uncle hearing the comment, "And you said… dream? What do you mean by *that*?"

"I don't know--" Bergas says, shrugging his shoulders.

It's true. He doesn't really know what he'd meant by it. It's hard enough to explain something when he'd been told all his life to keep as much about his secret.

"Well--" Draigus asks softly. There's an edge of annoyance in his voice because he's having a hard time believing a 'dream.'

"I dreamt it. I'm *not* lying--" Bergas hisses at the man opposite, then looks down.

Draigus stops his task of removing pearls and thinks for a moment before he answers, "I think there's something going on that *none* of our parents ever wants to speak about. Have you ever considered *why* your Uncle Hadukin remains without a life partner? I have my view. I think it's because of what he saw happen when he was my age--"

"What did he see?" Bergas whispers.

"I think you will need to *wait* until the day comes when he wants to tell you that himself--" Draigus replies, "But I've been told by him to teach you *all* my own skills before I'm to travel to the far southeast--"

"You're leaving?" Bergas asks, staring wide-eyed at the man.

"Yes, both Timorin and I are… We were told by--Well, by who

isn't important… Just know that something is going to happen, and *she* knows it--" Draigus says solemnly.

"She?" Bergas asks. Draigus leans forward, then after brief pause whispers, "The old woman--"

"Ohhh--" Bergas says as he leans back.

"--Wants us to go somewhere really, but your father and uncle shouldn't know about it. For us to go there to learn skills is just a ruse. Apparently, the journey will take us five years and then we'll meet someone who's very, very important," Draigus says. "His name isn't important, and I was told to tell you, is to make sure you always remember that the man with the wolf means is your friend. When you meet him, you listen to him every day--"

Bergas frowns about the mention of someone with a wolf. It's what he'd dreamt about…

"What's so important about being in the south in five years?" he asks hesitantly, avoiding the other part of the comment made which seems to relate to wolves.

"I guess you don't really know what the old woman was or is then?" Draigus whispers, "Alright, I may occasionally make fun of her but I get the feeling, that she's someone more important than most give her credit for. Something also is going on between her and Hadukin. He seems to know her. He and your father seem to care enough about her to have given the dwelling that belonged to their parents to her almost fifty years ago--"

Bergas stops his work and stares with mouth open wide at Draigus. "What?" he says after a few minutes.

"There are things you shouldn't dwell on with a mind so young as yours--" Draigus says softly.

"But I want to know--I dreamt about wolves. Why would I've done that?" Bergas blurts out.

"I don't know. I'm not privy to knowing things that were before or things that come after," Draigus says softly.

"What do you mean by that?" Bergas asks, snorting as he laughs in a way only sceptical boys can do. Draigus smiles but decides not to answer that question.

He'll know soon enough if what the old woman says is right--

Draigus observes the boy for a while as the boy seems to speed up the process of obtaining pearls.

Bergas realises suddenly from the comments he'd heard just moments earlier that the more pearls he gets while in the cave, the more time he will have with his father. It was never certain whether a person you loved would be there the day after, and he is hoping that he has many more years with his father, but something deep down also tells him that time was shorter than he'd thought possible until this moment.

It seems now that the old woman in the library knows something of what the future brings, and he wonders for a moment why she'd want to spend all her time surrounded with them rather than teaching him or others in the city what she knows. Bergas remembers how he'd reacted seeing all the books there, many of which seem so old, and had various dialects on them he's uncertain of.

Maybe I should ask my father about them someday…

Draigus knows in some ways why he's so sceptical of what the old woman stated to him about the journey she insisted he should make. His father lost a sister in the same fire that the old woman somehow survived. He never understands why his father is so determined to want to hold on to the idea that the will be better. But now this boy opposite of him reminds him why his father speaks in how he did, and why he keeps a white statue secured in a box inside a chest in the front room…

The emotions Bergas feels at this same moment, while the man is in a similar pensive mood, relate to the dream he'd been having. In it saw a wolf. But *one* specific wolf, and later seemingly his father, promised to show him wolves in the mountains above him.

I better just keep quiet about wolves and even more about these dreams I'm getting. Something is so odd about them. It's like they are a warning of some sort. Maybe I should just stay home rather than go to that damned harbour…

He doesn't know it yet, but it will be *other* reasons than an offer of teaching skills that will ultimately drive him to the harbour later. By then, Draigus and Timorin will already have departed. Bergas doesn't realise that a more tragic reason will cause him to feel guilt. It will be this that forces his own mind to go help there. Once there, he'll be in mortal danger within hours…

"I think I'm going now--" Draigus says softly, "I think Hadukin wants to head back to town, and I need to steer his boat. I *hope* to see you at the harbour in a few days from now--"

Bergas doesn't answer and stubbornly doesn't look up. He feels tears sting as he hears the man walk off grumbling under his breath…

CHAPTER SEVEN

"Your mother told me to teach you skills she felt you'd need. Never ask me *why* she asked or *what* will happen, but I'm going to teach the skills I think you'll need--" Jerid says quietly.

Bergas stops eating and looks up at his father. "Why is Mam so worried these days?" Bergas asks.

"She has *her* reasons--I cannot go into the specific reasons," Jerid says.

Bergas slumps his shoulders. He is silent for a few moments, then he looks up at his father, smiling.

"Maybe she's just worried because we weren't sure about how many of the pearls we could get--" Bergas says, and he tries to sound like he was being hopeful.

He hopes his father will believe that this is what he thinks.

Bergas smiles inwardly when he hears his father's answer, "I think you're right--" Jerid says.

Bergas pretends *not* to see the attempt by his father to hide the worry on his own face when the familiar worry frown flashes over his face as had done so for the last few months.

"Let's continue our trek…" Jerid says softly.

He gets up and helps the boy with strapping on the haversack he'd got for the boy before they'd gone on their trip.

When Bergas looks up at his father, he saw his father's smiling face, then his father placed a hand on his shoulder. "I shouldn't say this, and if your mother knew I did, she'd be furious with me, but please promise this. If something happened to me, will you always make sure you look after your mother for me? She is more vulnerable than she lets anyone, myself included, see. She told me things-- happened to her once. I cannot go into details of them, and never ask me about them, but something happened to her. I see in your own eyes you are certain of this too. If something happens, be a smart boy and *DO* what she tells you--"

Bergas swallows hard, then nods. Suddenly he feels a deep, overwhelming fear. "Papa, if I promise about that, will you promise to not tell her about me--" he whispers.

"In what way, son? What has happened?" Jerid asks, now frowning again, looking worried.

"I dreamt about wolves--I know you're going to show them to me, but I dreamt about them too. I don't know why--" Bergas whispers.

For a moment, he wonders if his father would become angry, but he looks up when he hears his father sigh audibly. "Perhaps with what your mother is, I should have realised much sooner that you may be the same--"

Jerid says nothing else but silently walks towards the scree at the foot of Northern Blades. After standing for a few minutes with a perplexed look on his face, Bergas does the same. He asks nothing. His mind already knows, he was just told the answer by his father in no uncertain terms, that he suspects his son to be the *same* as what his life partner of more than a decade is; that they *both* share the ability to know about things that will happen in the future. Emotions wash over Bergas as he thinks about the words, which spin themselves around his mind: *"Perhaps with what your mother is, I should have realised much sooner that you may be the same--"*

Is he telling me that Mam also dreams of wolves?

Bergas knows that beyond what his father just said, he'd get no further answers, ever. Not from his father, and not from his mother. He shrugs his shoulders and pays attention to his surroundings instead. They walk towards the scree that's about three hundred paces from the shore, where Jerid had landed on shore with the boat that he often uses for this sort of trips. Bergas glances back towards the boat for a moment, mostly to be sure it was still moored on the stony beachhead.

"It's not going anywhere--"

Bergas felt his heart jump in his chest when he hears his father speak. He looks ahead to see his father standing some fifty paces away, looking at him smiling, and then gets a wink that seems to show that his father knows what he is thinking about.

"Are you still thinking about your mother?" Jerid asks when Bergas catches up with him. Bergas shakes his head and looks down, but the silence around him makes him look up. It seems his father won't continue walking until they settle this matter--or so it seems. He nods quickly.

"I think you're worried about her because of what I told you, is that right?" Jerid asks.

Bergas nods again.

"And are you also worried about wolves?" Jerid now asks. "Yes, Papa--" Bergas whispers.

Jerid stoops down to look his son in his eyes. "I think you're worried about things you cannot control. *None* of us can--" Jerid says softly, "But the way you deal with it, is going to make you *strong*. Whatever happens, you have to remember this always. Both your mother and I love you, son, and we're *here*--"

Jerid gently places his broad hand over Bergas's chest and holds it there for a minute or so, before he removes. He lifts his hand and holds Bergas's face up by placing his hand under the boy's chin, then gently states, "I love you, son, *never* forget that. Whatever happens, you carry my love in your heart, always…"

"I love you too, Papa--" Bergas says softly.

He feels his eyes sting with tears. He knew both parents reassured him daily by that they both love him. Knowing that was making the feeling of loss that always followed the dreams so much more pronounced--especially those in which he'd see his father's upturned boat.

"Papa, can we go see the wolves, please…?" Bergas asks softly.

"Yes--Let's do that. And when we're halfway up that hill, we pause a while for some roasted ailep hound meat that your mother packed for us--" Jerid says, smiling weakly.

He gets up, and he does a quiet cursing, *Next time I should go for a sandy beach to kneel--*

* * *

J erid stops walking for a moment, then glances around for a suitable place for them to sit and eat. He feels Bergas's hand slide into his own, and the added weight of the boy against his left arm shows that the boy is more tired than perhaps he would want to admit to. Jerid glances down and smiles down at Bergas.

He's only an eleven-year-old boy, but he needs to know the skills of a grown man. Why did Emelyse even suggest to me to do this with the boy…?

CHAPTER EIGHT

Jerid sits down on the elongated stone overlooking a small green pasture. Mountain sheep scatter in all directions when the unfamiliar smells of the man and the boy enter their nostrils. The already skittish animals hesitate for moments, then walk off a bit more.

"Always watch them whenever you are in the mountains alone, Bergas, they will guide you to the paths used by the herders…" Jerid says softly.

Bergas nods, then he looks at the mountain sheep closer, trying to make a mental note of every movement they make now.

"Do you see that one there…?" Jerid asks. He points at the ewe with two lambs by her side, both darting around their mother to reach for her teats while she nervously keeps ascending the higher parts of the pasture.

Bergas nods, "How old are they?" he asks.

"A season past birthing--" Jerid replies. "They'll leave her in another season from now--"

"Is that the same with all animals?" Bergas realises there's perhaps a reason *why* his father mentioned this and said this in relation to what they'd talked about earlier in the day.

"The wolves we're going to see are different in their birthing. They *do* the care of their young in a group," Jerid continues. "The mother is helped by aunts and sisters to give milk to the offspring, and then she carries them with her far up into the highest parts of the mountains…"

Jerid points up to the peaks of the Northern Blades, which for the most part keep themselves hidden from view with perpetual cloud cover, only ever revealing their true height with an occasional cloud bursting. They explained to Bergas before what the cloud burstings are. It's when warmer air rushes towards the mountain and pushes the colder snow-filled clouds around the mountain peaks apart.

"Won't the pups be cold up there?" he asks, with a touch of worry clear in his voice.

"Nooo, they adapt fast to cold weather, and their mother's milk gives them the warmth and strength the cope--" Jerid answers.

"I guess they keep warm as well when they are carried up--" Bergas smiles at his father. An approving nod from his father shows he came to a pleasant conclusion.

"How far do the mountains go?" Bergas asks now.

"They go all the way to a region called Zehar, but I know nothing of that region other than that my father always warned me *never* to go there--" Jerid now sounds as stern as he does, whenever he felt a need to chastise Bergas. "He said that something goes on there that makes it *too* dangerous for everyone--"

Bergas swallows hard, then nods. He realises that his father is warning him about something, or perhaps someone…

* * *

"Watch out here… these rocks will be slippery--" Jerid points at the rocky path to the left of a waterfall which trickles down the slope in almost slow motion.

This waterfall appeared different from the waterfall that's located north of their house where Bergas would play in summer with other children from the city. It was during the previous year's visit to the waterfall the boy met a girl called Elennia, and they had talked. It was Elennia who suggested to him he should go on this trip with his father when Bergas said to her he wasn't sure about wanting to go.

She'd told Bergas about this waterfall, saying her father had taken her to see it two years earlier. Bergas smiles when he realises how accurate her description of it had been.

"I think Elennia told me about this--" Bergas says, smiling for a moment.

"Is that one of your friends?" Jerid asks.

Bergas nods.

But Jerid smiles knowingly, seeing the change in colour on his son's face. He keeps silent and won't do in that moment what most fathers will do. He remembers when his father and also his older brother Hadukin had teased about him liking a girl in the city. Hadukin had looked at him with a teasing smile when he'd arrived in town with Emelyse declaring her as his 'promised.'

I guess he's an older brother who never can stop teasing me, but I guess I get enough chances to do the same to him as well, Jerid smirks for a moment at the memory and turning his face so not to make his son think that the thought was about him.

"Papa, what's *that?*"

Jerid turns and looks in the direction where Bergas is pointing. He squints his eyes against the glare of the sun reflecting off the snowy surface above them.

"What are you looking at, son?" he asks a moment later.

"I think I saw something moving near that dark rock--or something, not sure if that's a rock or not--" Bergas answers.

Jerid looks at the landscape for several minutes, while Bergas glances back and forth from where he'd seen a shape of something to his father--mostly to see if his father *would* believe him. He bites his lip and feels a knot of nervousness in his stomach for several moments.

"Yes, there it is--" Jerid says softly and suddenly.

It makes Bergas jump.

"I think you spotted one of the wolves. It's a loner by the look of it. A young male," he adds a moment later.

Jerid squats down next to the boy and points to a rocky outcrop somewhat further away from where the boy had seen the beast.

"I think it has seen us and decided to run off--" Jerid whispers, while pointing at the outcrop with an outstretched arm, "Do you see it…?" he asks.

Bergas looks in the direction his father points, then sees the animal. It's not *too* large, somewhat darker than grey, and from the shape, it's obviously a male--if he'd compare this animal with ailep hounds that he'd hunted with his father a few times.

"Is that a young wolf?" Bergas whispers.

"It is--" Jerid replies.

"Are the ones we're going to see bigger, then?" Bergas asks next.

"They are, son, It will be another day or so before we're there--" Jerid replies.

They walk on, now constantly stopping to see if the wolf really had been a loner, but no other animals were visible in any direction.

It was an hour later when they arrive at the chasm where reality for Bergas would change. He's told of Mountain Ghost by his father while watching the wolves on the mountain above them…

CHAPTER NINE

Jerid points across the chasm towards where he'd spotted movement moments earlier. Bergas follows his motion with his gaze, then he sees the group of large grey wolves.

"Oooh, they're big--" Bergas whispers.

"Yes, they *are*. Your mother told me to show them. She says it'll help you later, though I cannot explain how or why--" Jerid explains.

Bergas nods.

"They say that 'Mountain Ghost' was even bigger. Maybe even the biggest of her kind--" Jerid whispers.

"You're saying that the wolf was female?" Bergas asks.

"Yes, she was. And Darius used her," Jerid replies.

"Who is that?" Bergas asks.

"It's one of the most important people for you to remember for the rest of your life--" Jerid whispers back, "He's the one who helped make the whole of Keldarra safe again--he drove the northern invaders away--"

"Oooh, I see--" Bergas whispers. "And these wolves are the same type of wolf as Mountain Ghost?"

"Very likely the *same* group of wolves or her offspring even, with at least some of them having ten individual families that usually live together--" Jerid explains. "At least half of the largest one can be of the same line of wolves that made Mountain Ghost the size she was. It's her size that Darius saw. He knew the northern invaders had used wolves for riding to be more intimidating to those they enslaved. The people of this land called it Keltana once. It became known by a name that means 'bound to Queltha' where we get the current name Keldarra from, though I am uncertain of how it will have sounded in the dialect where the name was first voiced by those people using it some two thousand years ago--"

"So, the dialect we speak isn't the only one then?" Bergas asks softly.

"No, it's one of perhaps twenty or thirty based on the six prominent ones they spoke in the earliest days of the occupation by the northern invaders. The 'language' that those calling themselves 'Keltana's Children' was lost soon after they arrived. Those people in 'The Old Days' didn't refer to themselves as Keltanians, or similar, but called themselves that according to what Jarryca told my mother once."

"And the language was gone because of them forbidding it, I guess?" Bergas asks.

"That's correct…" Jerid replies.

"So, when this Darius helped to free us, why didn't we use the language again?" Bergas asks.

"I think we forgot how to. The oldest books in Jarryca's library are written only in various dialects. It means they were written *long* after that language of Keltana's Children was lost," Jerid answers.

"I wish I could have seen Darius on Mountain Ghost--" Bergas says.

"I think *many* now wish it. At the least, it would have meant that the Wolf Riders wouldn't feel so empowered to do their own version of copying the northern invaders."

Jerid looks grim as he speaks the words, and he also frowns momentarily as the answer did possibly cause him to be saying things the boy could interpret that as a warning.

"How many wolves are there in total up there?" Bergas asks, apparently oblivious of the latter part of Jerid's words.

Jerid was silent for about five minutes, then replies, "I think at least twenty in total here, but you never know how many there are really as most of the youngest wolves and pups keep out of sight-- and you see *that* one there?"

Bergas looks to where his father points, then he nods.

"That's the matriarch of the entire group. She's the group's leader. She'll tell them to go away if *she* smells our scent. We're currently upwind from them so it will be harder for them to perceive that we're here," Jerid says, "But wind can change direction fast up here, and they can smell many times better than we ever can. *She* could know already and being cautious be alert."

Bergas nods again and then observes the matriarch wolf once again. "Was Mountain Ghost a matriarch, perhaps?"

"Considering her apparent size, and comparing it with this wolf, she could have been--" Jerid says and nods confirmation of the assessment.

"Can we go closer?" Bergas whispers, "Even if they end up going away I want to try it--"

"We can, but if they go, it may take us a while to find more of them--"

They get up, slowly, and watch the wolves for any movement that may show they've been noticed. Bergas copied his father's motions. He looks up at his father and sees him holding a finger over his mouth. He nods. Jerid motions to the boy to follow him. Bergas copies his father's every move to make sure they could get closer to the wolves. He keeps darting glances at them to make sure the group they'd been watching was still sitting in the small clearing across the chasm. To him, it almost seemed that the wolf his father had pointed out as the matriarch was watching them…

"Papa, does she know we're here…?" Bergas whispers.

Jerid glances towards the animals, and notes they're circling closer to the matriarch and that she stands so much taller than before.

"Maybe it's best if we wait to see what they'll do--" he replies softly.

Bergas nods and stops walking when his father stops.

"Lets back up really slowly--" Jerid says.

"Alright, Papa--" Bergas whispers. He now feels fearful.

If these are similar wolves as the Wolf Riders used, they may now be in danger. It's very telling too. If the warning he'd received from Draigus, is one that shows that the dreams about the wolves are about what life is possibly like as a Wolf Rider, then neither of them are equipped enough to deal with a group of snarling wolves aren't even controlled by a man. As young as he is, Bergas sees the danger…

As the distance grows larger, the overwhelming feeling of foreboding leaves Bergas, and he stands panting in the same spot as he'd been running for a time. Tears stream down both cheeks. Fear grips his mind, and he stares at his father with two round eyes. Jerid notices something wrong with the boy and after first asserting that the wolves are gone, he squats down to the boy and places a hand on his left shoulder and looks into the boy's eyes for a time…

CHAPTER TEN

Jerid waits for a few minutes before he speaks, "I thought you looked uncertain while you sat in the boat working on collecting the pearls."

He looks searchingly over the boy's face, even wiping some wetness from the boy's face with a roughened thumb, "What's wrong, son?"

Instead of answering, Bergas throws himself against Jerid, and a moment later he's sobbing loud. "I didn't mean to…" Bergas says between sobs, "I *know* I need to be careful…"

"What do you *mean*, Bergas?" Jerid asks.

He holds his son by his shoulders at arm's length. He looks closely at Bergas. The boy's face shows fear. Not the fear that a boy may show for what punishment a father could deal out, though Jerid is always sparing with his compared to other parents in the city, but the fear of a boy who knows too much about something terrible.

"What *do* you *mean*?" Jerid asks again; this time more forceful. His forceful question is answered by another sob. "If you don't tell me, I cannot try to help you cope with whatever it is…" Jerid says using a gentler tone.

"I had dreams…" Bergas whispers.

"Dreams… what *do* you mean, son?" Jerid asks.

"Dreams where things seem to show…" Bergas says hesitantly.

Jerid frowns as his mind suddenly realises with clarity what Bergas says to him so hesitantly. *Did he have dreams that are like those that plague Emelyse's mind from time to time,* he thinks, *I think I need to talk with Bergas so he knows not to tell anyone in the city about these dreams, and least of all to tell his mother of them…*

Bergas looks at his father, considering in his mind what and how much to say now. He thought his father *wanted* to know, but now he wasn't certain how to explain.

"I spoke with Draigus, who suggested I should tell you…" he says.

He shouldn't have told that to the man, Jerid thinks, but then he remembers that his brother had stated the man was going on a journey of some sort.

Jerid ignores the fact he just got told that more than himself know of the dreams his son seems to have, and keep asking questions to find out why, how and about what. The 'what' part was the most important part to determine as Bergas started acting in this odd way since arriving here with him where the wolves are.

The wolves…, he thinks.

He glances sideways towards where the large pack was, but the field beyond the chasm was empty now. The sound of Bergas crying spooked them in the end, and that the matriarch sent her pack back to the higher reaches of the mountain range.

He looks down at Bergas and notes that he *too* is looking towards where the wolves had been. The disappointment is clear on the boy's face. But there's also some relief on the boy's face, which contorts the boy's face into an odd mixture of emotions.

"We'll find the wolves after we've talked. I promise…" Jerid says softly.

Bergas nods.

"I suggest we make camp here. It's getting late in the day, the trek to where we *will* find the wolves again is long," Jerid suggests. "You choose where…" he adds encouragingly.

Bergas smiles weakly, but he smiles. He glances around in all directions. After a few minutes of indecision, Bergas points to the east at a small piece of pasture under a tree with a large boulder behind the tree.

"There…!" Bergas says hesitantly.

"Alright, we make camp there…" Jerid says, again using an encouraging tone.

The encouragement causes Bergas's smile to become broader.

They lift their haversacks from the ground and walk single file towards the tree.

* * *

"The soup is ready--" Jerid calls out.

"I'll be there shortly, Papa--" Bergas calls back. He'd gone to collect more wood for the campfire he'd help his father build. After their long discussion about the dreams Bergas is having, they'd agreed to make the rest of their journey all about fun, and Jerid ends up reassuring his son that Bergas wants to discuss anything with him to just tell him.

"I will, Papa, I promise--"

Neither knows yet that these words will end up haunting them. It will haunt one person in his last moments, and the other in the dangerous situation he'd find himself in less than a year later…

"Papa, I found a beautiful stone."

Bergas approaches the camp with a large bundle in his arms and holding a stone in his right hand. He places the wood near the campfire, then he walks to his father and hands over the stone. Jerid looks at the stone.

"I think you found a stone from before the Eye of Waves existed--" Jerid grins.

"What is the Eye of Waves?"

"You recall us going to the coast north of Azaquina...?" Jerid asks while he uses some water to wash the dirt off the stone.

"Yes, I do--" Bergas replies.

"That was the Eye of Waves we visited--" Jerid says.

"Oh right, I forgot its name--" Bergas whispers.

"You were still young. Only around five or six years old. Mother was with us--"

"Oooh, now I remember it--" Bergas says enthusiastically.

"Well then, *this* stone has an imprint on it," Jerid says, "Look just here in the light of the flames--"

Bergas sits down in front of his father, and bends towards the stone and looks at what his father points at.

"What's that?"

"That's evidence of a time of *many* thousands of years ago-- much longer ago than The Old Days, even longer than the old nation called Keltana existed--is when *this* animal that made this imprint existed. Some say that in the time of Keltana they knew what these were, but that they forgot the knowledge when the northern invaders came," Jerid explains, "I can tell by the imprint it was a sea animal, but there's no way to know what sort of animal it was--"

"Maybe it's a crustacean, like the ones we got the pearls from--" Bergas suggests.

"That's a very reasonable suggestion--"

"Papa, can you tell me more about when they called the land Keltana?"

"I can only tell you what *my* father taught me. There's another person in Azaquina, who knows a *lot* more than I do, and I suggest you ask *her* about it more when you get the chance. She knows *more* than most, and my father learned from her what he knew, and then he told me. I think I'll be spending the rest of this night telling the retellings about Keltana, so let's make fresh tea to drink and then I get started--"

* * *

"“You always *need* to keep quiet about what you told me. Bergas, can you promise me that?” Jerid asks, looking at his sternest.

“I won't tell her, Papa--”

“And whatever happens, always *remember* everything I taught you, even *if* the dreams come true--”

“I won't--” Bergas whispers.

CHAPTER ELEVEN

Jerid glances over his shoulder to ensure that Bergas was keeping up. He'd left Bergas at the camp for a time on his own to go for a quick trek on his own to search for where the wolves had relocated themselves. Suddenly he found it extremely important that Bergas *should* see them. He'd arrived back at the camp, and to the smell of a broth being cooked, just past mid-morning. It made him realise at that moment that the boy knew how to feed himself.

"That smells delicious--" Jerid calls out, and by the motion of the boy turning, then smiling broadly at him, and then rushing towards him for a hug, it's obvious that Bergas did worry about his father's absence but that he'd made the broth as a way to distract himself from his worry.

"I hope it was alright for me to do it--"

"Of course. I'm glad you made it. I'm starving--" Jerid smiles at the boy.

The relief on the boy's face is evident, but Jerid decides not to comment on it.

"Once we've eaten we can go to where I spotted the wolves--" he says instead.

"The broth is almost ready, Papa. Maybe another thirty minutes cooking--" Bergas says.

Jerid has to smile at the way Bergas is almost trying to will the food to cook faster by the way he sits back down and is now staring intently at the top of the cooking pot, where the slowly bubbling mixture is visible. He smiles. It's now so obvious that Bergas is a miniature version of Emelyse because she *too* has the same impatience when it comes to food being cooked.

Jerid sits down on a boulder opposite of Bergas and inhales for a moment to get an idea what the food may taste like. He could smell ailep hound meat, and glances at his haversack. It was open and Jerid guesses that Bergas decided to check it for additional supplies for a meal while he was gone.

"Do you remember what I told you before about Mountain Ghost?" Jerid asks. Bergas thought for a moment then he nods.

"One of the wolves I *saw* while I was looking for them could be as big as *that* wolf apparently has been," Jerid continues.

"Oooh--and we're going to see *that* one?" Bergas asks with a hopeful edge to his voice. Jerid nods solemnly. There's now a big grin on Bergas's face. He gets up, rushes to his haversack and retrieves two bowls from which they could eat, and from a side-pocket, in Jerid's haversack, he gets two spoons.

He places both near the pot of cooking broth then Jerid has to grin when he hears Bergas mumbling, "Get ready, get ready, please get ready--"

Jerid realises that Bergas will want to go as soon as possible so he decides to lend a hand in cooking. He gets up, pretending, of course, that he hasn't heard Bergas, he walks to the cook pot and picks up the spoon beside it apparently to 'taste.'

"Hmm, that tastes ready. I think you need to check, Bergas, you know your old father isn't a good judge in these matters--" Jerid hands Bergas the spoon, and the boy now needs to taste too. "I think I can serve it out *now*--" he says softly.

"Then *do* that, please--" Jerid says as he walks back to the boulder he'd been sitting on. *This means we can go much sooner to view the wolves,* he thinks at the same time.

Jerid takes the bowl handed to it, and for a moment again smells the wholesome aroma coming from it. It did smell good. He smiles then starts eating the broth.

"I hope you like it, Papa."

Jerid nods silently but smiles broadly at his son.

"When we go, can you just tell me which direction we should go, and let me work out what route to take?" Bergas asks softly but shyly.

"That sounds like a good plan, Bergas," Jerid says approvingly, "It will help you learn more about the wilderness and one day it can serve you well when that information will lead you back home. And yes, it's something your mother said, but again I cannot go into the details of why she said this, but I think you deserve honesty and therefore I will explain as much as I can--but promise me you never ever will question your mother. I'm certain that any such question will be met with the same 'I'll tell you one day' that your old father gets each time--"

Bergas stops eating and stares at his father in shock. He'd received some explanation earlier, but this statement made it clear that his father had been doing a lot of thinking about what could happen, and perhaps also had been thinking about the implications of what Bergas had told him of the dreams he'd experienced. He quickly looks down again uncertain of everything now.

Bergas is silent for several minutes. "Papa--" he says softly.

No answer comes from his father.

"*Papa--*" Bergas repeats with some force.

"Yes, son," Jerid replies softly, his voice cracking under the emotion he was obviously feeling.

"I think I *know* what Mam meant with what she said--" Bergas says softly.

Jerid looks up and sees his son looking at him intently. No worry, sadness or anger is evident in his son's face, and it seemed a resolute expression of determination has replaced it all.

"I think I know she means that whatever happens, she'll tell me later about it. I just have to *wait* for the right day to come for it. The dreams also explained that to me--" Bergas continues.

"You now sound just like your mother--" Jerid blurts out.

"You mentioned I'm like her with the cooking. I heard you," Bergas says. "If I'm the same as her with that, I'm certain I'm the same in *other* ways too--"

Bergas decides to refrain from saying how, but the change in expression on his father's father indicates that Jerid realises the implications of what his son is saying--or at a minimum implying.

"I think you're right," Jerid says after several minutes of silence. "But *do* promise me that you won't ask her that question until you are much older--"

"I think I'm meant to wait for an answer to *all* my questions--" Bergas replies. "It's something that I heard Jarryca say to Mam. She said that dreams of wolves mean more than just a warning for danger. She's convinced that it also tells that the bad people on their wolves *will* be stopped one day. I believe my dreams are about that--"

CHAPTER TWELVE

Bergas walks ahead of his father on this leg of their journey through the Northern Blades. Jerid had suggested that it would make the boy more capable of judging where to step, and also which way to go in the wilderness. Bergas stops for a moment and looks at the two paths he saw ahead. Jerid steps in beside his son and watches his face as a game of decision-making clouds it for several moments.

"Papa, I'm uncertain--" Bergas says after a few minutes.

"We're never certain, son," Jerid responds, "The only ones who are, are those with an eye on what can happen in the future."

"Like Mam…?"

"Like Mam…" Jerid replies, "But even *she* isn't ever certain of the future. She says there's *another* of her kind needed to be *certain* of what the future brings with all certainty, and most of those, who can do such things, have vanished now."

Bergas nods, then he is silent for a while, and Jerid lets him alone with whatever thoughts were running through his mind for a while, then speaks again.

"I'm not one who knows of such matters, such as the ones that your mother spoke to me about, but she always is certain of one thing," Jerid continues. "She says that there will come a day when she meets a woman sitting on a wolf, and when that day comes that's the day when the future that was told so long ago *will* happen--"

"I've seen a woman on a wolf too--"

"If you have, then keep onto that image as an image of hope, son. Because whatever happens, it's something foretold many thousands of years ago, even. It's a message of peace and hope for this land that they called Keltana once, long ago."

"I remember the words told that came apparently from Jarryca. She told Draigus to tell it to me."

"If Jarryca meant for you to get that message, then make sure you *do* what she said in it. You said it was a message for a man riding on a wolf, right?"

"She apparently said that I would meet him soon after I was--" Bergas says, but he decides not to end the sentence as telling it could cause such things to happen.

"I understand. Don't worry, as I told your mother. *Nothing* is going to happen," Jerid replies reassuringly.

But it will happen, Bergas thinks, *but I will not tell him--*

"Can we go this way?" Bergas points to the right-hand path.
"You're deciding the route there, so if that's the way you want to go, then that way we shall go," Jerid replies. "Either path brings us closer to them. 'Left' would get us to 'south' of where *they* are, but 'right' will be better because we'll be above them and looking down is so much easier than looking up."

Bergas smiles, then he turns and walks towards the right path, only hesitating for a moment which Jerid notes but not comments on.

The boy needs to trust his own decisions. That's the only way he'll cope with what Emelyse says will happen to him--

* * *

"It's over that ridge, Bergas--" Jerid says as he points to the south-east.

Bergas grins at the prospect of seeing wolves soon. His apparent enthusiasm rubs off on Jerid, who feels a renewed bounce in his own step. The climb to the ridge was steep, both for someone old as himself and even more for someone as young as Bergas.

But Jerid had learnt from his own father from a young age that certain actions that a boy, or girl *too*, does during their younger years will build a resistance in the muscles of such a person. Emelyse is *proof* of this being true. He's the only person in the city who knows she'd travelled for *more* years than most know. She'd even kept this information from one *other* she trusted in the city--Jarryca.

Bergas stops for a moment, and Jerid sees that the boy seems to listen, "Are you listening to see if they're really there?"

"Yes, Papa, but I'm doing it, so I always will recognise the sound of approaching wolves--for later--" Bergas says solemnly.

"Then tell me, son, *do* you hear them there?" Jerid asks, sounding as solemnly.

"Yes, I think so," Bergas says softly, "But I don't know how many."

"When I was here yesterday, I saw ten of them," Jerid says. "They were on the other side of *that* ridge."

"Ten!" Bergas blurts out.

"Yes, ten," Jerid responds.

"Are you certain it's safe for us to see them, Papa?"

"Yes, I'm certain," Jerid says somewhat hesitantly.

Bergas glances once at his father, quickly so he wouldn't notice. Something about what his father said felt ominous suddenly.

"I *want* to see them--" Bergas tries to sound like an unruly, sullen child rather than one, who was slightly more than a year and a season from First Rites.

In his dreams, Bergas had seen himself being taken in the autumn season, and right now it was late summer. There's some uncertainty why he can't see recent dreams, but he'd seen them. He could still remember the warning given by Draigus *not* to tell his father of the dreams he saw.

They give a warning while the man sat opposite of him in a boat, still talking while he showed anger.

"A lot more is going on than your young mind knows or understands, and a day could come when the words of a mother get ignored. Heed my warning, son of my master's cousin, you're the pawn in a game of war that none even realises is going on. One person knows. She's Jarryca. But her words are forgotten or

ignored now and have been for twice as long as I've been alive. Someone means to cause much more harm to this world who comes from the east. If the men on wolves come, you need to hide. But Jarryca says you're the one who'll start stirrings in the mind of the one who'll bring the girl who'll help to end all this. Whatever your father and mother say, ignore it. Listen to Jarryca's words instead. Hide when they come, but let yourself taken. She says that the one to start the salvation of this world will be saving you from boys of your own age who mean to be as cruel as their own abductors."

CHAPTER THIRTEEN

"We *need* to go home. Mother awaits us."

It's obvious from the upset on his face that Bergas wanted to stay a lot longer in the Northern Blades. He rushes to his father and hugs him tightly and he gets a hug back from his father in return, "Thank you for bringing me here, Papa. I enjoyed the trip--"

"We can go to the other mountains northeast of where we live, if you want to do that. It's a much longer trip, and it's a place your mother wants you to see. She says that knowing about. Well, what it is isn't really important. What *is* important is that you get to spend *more* time with your old father?"

"What are those mountains called?"

"They're called 'Upper Plains.' The furthest northeastern stretch is the place where a *very* important battle took place, and one of the last battles for which they needed Darius and Mountain Ghost..."

"Did they die there?" Bergas feels a knot of worry for the unknown man from the past.

"No, they lived a long life and helped found many of the cities of Keldarra. But Jarryca is the one to ask such things, and perhaps you should *ask* her about this city as well," Jerid replies.

"I'll ask her when I next go to the library with Mam."

"I think it's *best* you wait for a while, to let things settle around here *first* before you ask. I cannot tell you what's going on, but Jarryca said to *me,* that she'll tell you after your First Rites as a gift."

"Alright, Papa. I promise--"

I wish there was a way not to tell any of this to my son, but it seems Draigus already did some damage. I best make sure it goes no further. All of us are pawns in some sort of scheme for war. I hope that war will never come. Or at least that my son is safe at home away from it all, he thinks, but Jerid knows he can't stop a future already seen by his life partner.

He has seen the images too - images of his son being carried away by a man with dirty blond hair. With another man with black hair, laughing menacing at his son…

"Let's repack everything for an easier trek home," Jerid says gently. "And let's not make that journey a hasty one so I can teach more of what you surely will need to know for the days, that will come our way."

* * *

Bergas looks in both directions of the ditch in the landscape. He's checking it for the features his father had told him about moments earlier.

"There--" Bergas sees a narrow carved stairway in the embankment's side. "Is that it, Papa?"

"Yes, son. That's a thief's stairs--" Jerid responds as he squats down beside the boy.

"What are they for, Papa?"

"There's a retelling from almost eight hundred years ago that's linked to them. It's a retelling from far in the east," Jerid begins. "It's your mother, in fact, who told me about this retelling saying that her mother and her mother's mother told her about it. It's the retelling of a girl thief, and she lived in a very strange city--"

"How strange?"

As an answer, Jerid picks up a few short branches, and he places them in the ground, with the pointed end up, with them showing an arched row of them.

"The city where the girl thief lived looks like this--" he states, pointing at the sticks.
"You mean on top of tall sticks?"
"No, on rocks that raised themselves from the ocean, which have existed for tens of thousands of years. According to your mother, her city is almost as old as that city."

Jerid points again at the sticks. "She said that a long bridge connects the largest northern of these with the mainland, with the rest of Keldarra," Jerid explains, and draws a line in the sandy soil underfoot representing where the bridge could be. "In the retelling, the bridge is so long, that it takes a *half* day to cross it from end to end. But this one here is where the girl thief is from, and she's *the reason* your mother's skill is so important. She discovered that it existed. She and two of her friends in fact--"

"How did they discover it?"

"Your mother says that according to the retelling something happened almost eight hundred years ago, and they placed the girl thief in permanent servitude, and during the first years of that fate, she discovered a crystal in a cave in the south," Jerid explains. "The retelling explains that evil men on these islands were searching for the crystal, as they knew it to be important. But none know why and how it's that they wanted the crystal."

"It sounds like a sad retelling--"

"It was a sad retelling, but according to your mother the girl ended up in the city where your mother comes from, but do *not* ask your mother about it, and do *not* say to her ever I told you this retelling," Jerid says, putting a hand on the shoulder of Bergas and gripping it with some force for a moment.

"I won't. I promise--" Bergas cringes somewhat under the pressure his father is asserting on him.

However, Jerid realises now that with the chance of his life partner's dreams becoming true, the boy should have to learn to deal with the idea that somethings people were less gentle with him.

"I'll explain more while we walk home. It's not a safe region here. The evil city where the men on wolves come from, lies south east of here--some three weeks walking away. I suggest that you *never* come near it no matter what. Its inhabitants will have sport with you in many cruel ways."

Bergas decides not to ask any more questions, but looks towards the direction that his father had pointed, while he tries to listen for the sound of one specific animal--a wolf...!

CHAPTER FOURTEEN

Emelyse feels relief when a small boat, with father and son seated side by side, comes into view.

This is NOT the day it will happen, Emelyse bites her lip momentarily before she puts her face in a neutral stance. *Neither can ever know of the dreams I had with them gone. Not them, not anyone else--*

She knows *what* events her mind speaks of when the words echo through her mind. The tension she'd felt for all the last few days, while father and son had been away, now leaves her body and she feels the need to straighten up and to smile for the sake of her son who might worry if she looks upset.

Emelyse doesn't realise in that small moment of despair she's feeling, as she watches the small boat with Jerid and Bergas approaching, that both man and boy glance quickly at one another, each with a telling question on their faces, "What is the matter with her?"

Father and son quickly set about doing things on the boat to prevent Emelyse from noticing they'd noticed her facial expression.

"Pick up the rope, and throw it to that man up there, Bergas."

Jerid points at the coil of rope at the stern of the boat. Bergas nods and rushes to the rope his father had pointed to. He picks it up, then looks up at the pier above him, where he sees one man motion at him; obviously showing to him to throw the rope towards him. It takes Bergas six tries before he throws the rope up high enough for the waiting man to take hold of it--even with the added effort of lying flat on his stomach.

Knowing smiles are clear on every man's face--even on that of Jerid--but he shakes his head ever so gently, to make sure none of the men there will laugh. He doesn't want Bergas to feel ridiculed after asking him if he could try to do the task.

The boy shouldn't endure bullying now, because later he'd be weaker.

"Papa--"
"Yes, son," Jerid says then he smiles gently.
"Are you sad?" Bergas whispers.
"I'm sad, but not for the reasons you may think," Jerid whispers back.

Bergas frowns a moment, then nods, saying again, "I won't tell--"

"Tell who?"
"Won't tell Mam--"
"I know you won't. I *trust* you, son--" Jerid says softly.

He looks at his son, and for the first time, he notices how much older the boy seems in his behaviour. No longer did Bergas behave as the unruly child that had been so reluctant to help during the trip to the cave for pearl collecting. Here's a boy who looked at him for guidance to see what he'd want to say or do…

Bergas had been thinking long about the discussions he'd been having with his father on this trip, and somewhere halfway down the Bay of Whispers decided to *pretend* that nothing is wrong so neither parent will show any further worry about him. He smiles, knowing that neither parent will realise how much *more* he understands or knows of what's going on around him. Even so, the worrying images of his father behind him, drifting dead in the ocean, remain…

One thought now remains in his mind as Bergas walks behind his parents towards home, *I'm going to test them to see how much I can push them to find out the truth about me. To find out about where Mam came from…*

* * *

"Mam, can I visit my friends at the nearby house?" Bergas rushes into the cooking room, where Emelyse is busy unpacking the cooking pot, plates and cutlery that his father and he had used during their travel.

119

"You need to be home *early* this evening to rest. Your father plans to take you into town tomorrow," Emelyse answers.

"I'll be back before you serve out the evening meal. I promise I will…"

Emelyse just nods and smiles for the briefest moment as she hears footsteps rushing towards the front door, a door slam, then listens to running feet until they disappear in the distance.

"Emelyse, can you help me in the workshop?" Jerid's voice calls out a moment later.

"I'll be there shortly," she answers.

* * *

Elennia calls out, grinning, "Bergas, you came--"

"Yes, my father said it's alright for me to visit, then told me to ask Mam too. But she told me it's alright too," Bergas answers, smiling back at the girl who is a year younger. "My father said we're going up into these mountains next--"

"Did you see the waterfall I mentioned?"

"Yes, I asked Papa if I could see it. It's so much bigger than I imagined," Bergas answers.

Bergas smiles a moment, then takes Elennia's hand, saying, "Let's look at the city from up there."

He points north with his other hand.

"I'd love that. But we need to wait a bit. My brother said he wanted to come too, and he had to help Papa--"

"We wait then. Let's sit there to wait."

Bergas walks with Elennia to a couple of boulders next to the footpath and brushes his hand over the left one. Elennia smiles at him, then she sits down. Bergas sits down next to her.

"Have you been into these mountains with your father?" He points east.

"No, Papa says they're too dangerous. He says they're haunted by ghosts from the past, from some sort of battle that happened there," Elennia replies. "He says there are wolves there."

"My father told me about that battle. Only a bit. What your father said is true, but I think that they did the battle to make Keldarra free again. There's a man, who lived long ago named Darius. He rode a wolf and created the Wolf Masters. He was a brave person--"

"But what of those they call Wolf Riders?" Elennia asks, panic clear in her voice.

"I'm uncertain, but I think something similar to what Darius did so long ago, may happen now to make the land free from them too. To bring the peace we knew three thousand years ago *back* to the land."

I won't tell her what my role is in it. Not yet, perhaps never--, Bergas thinks, just as Elennia's brother arrives with a dozen others.

He has fun instead staying pensive over a future he cannot alter…

CHAPTER FIFTEEN

Bergas follows his father as they climb higher into the eastern mountain range. This time they were visiting Upper Plains, and the boy had received the *same* explanation as before that his mother *wants* him to know about them. They'd been travelling for almost a month, when they arrive at the first of the ancient massive buildings still standing in Upper Plains, always serving as a reminder of times gone by when their presence was a necessity.

Bergas looks around because it had become clear very soon after they'd set off that the landscape here was nothing like that of the Northern Blades. Although this landscape was lower than the western mountain, it seemed to possess a perpetual feeling of bleakness to it. Unlike the much higher western mountain range, the snow here had melted during the spring and summer months, and whereas on the Northern Blades snow had already started even though it was the end of the summer still, here the landscape is as green as the pastures that surround Azaquina.

But that's where the comparison ended in the mind of a young boy following his father on a trek through a terrain he'd been forbidden to ask about whenever it was mentioned his mother came from the east, and that he'd been forbidden to explore at any time before. But *now* his father was bringing him here on his mother's insistence.

"Papa, where are we going?" Bergas asks shyly. "I know you said you wanted me to see here, but it seems now you want me to see something specific--"

"I want you to see two things. One of them is just ahead, but the other will become visible in a few more weeks of the journey," Jerid says solemnly. "I know I've said it perhaps a thousand times already but--"

"… mother wants me to see it…" Bergas interjects.

However, this time his voice doesn't sound annoyed, angry or bored. Jerid raises an eyebrow because if he doesn't know better, Bergas is almost trying to imitate his mother.

"Is there a reason you're speaking in this way?" he asks sternly. "I don't think I *ever* heard you speak against your mother in anger. I thought you love her--"

"I love her, but you and Mam tell this *same* thing so often, and--" Bergas explains. He shuts up then, uncertain to say his thoughts.
"I think you share your mother's worry, is that it?"
"Yes, a bit, but--" Bergas answers, then stops talking again.

"But?"

"I worry because I dream not only of wolves but of both of you as well," Bergas whispers.
"Dream of *us*, how?" Jerid asks, now with worry clear in his own voice.
"I keep seeing you go on a boat, then I see Mam sad, like you're leaving us, and never coming back--" Bergas answers.

Bergas leaves out the part of seeing his father drifting upturned in the ocean.

"I love your mother. I'm not going anywhere."

Jerid squats down and takes Bergas in his arms, and Bergas reciprocates the act by placing his own arms around Jerid's neck.

In the next moment, a flood of tears escapes his eyes. Jerid holds him silently so that the apparent sorrow his son seems to feel can leave his body by itself.

It seems something is causing Bergas to feel this way. Maybe the boy knows more than either his mother or I ever thought possible. But I cannot tell Emelyse that the boy suspects and I cannot allow Bergas to realise that I know a lot more about how he feels than I have told him so far--Dammit, so many secrets and all caused by an enemy we're trying to protect him from. And even more of them caused by the unknown enemy Emelyse had to flee from--

After about five minutes, Bergas stops crying, and Jerid lets go of him. Jerid looks at his son's face streaked with tears, at the boy's red eyes, the fear that shows in those eyes. It confirms very much what he'd been thinking.

"I know that things will become tough for you. And perhaps painful beyond measure--I think I understand what you are trying to say without actually telling me. And I've decided I will not shield you from it. But remember this, son, *whatever* happens in the future, there's a future beyond it. No, don't speak, just listen to me--"

Jerid places a hand over Bergas's mouth for a moment, then removes it when he sees the boy nod.

"I know something will happen to me. No, your mother didn't tell me," Jerid continues, "But I see in your eyes you know the same. I know I won't be in your life for much longer. Do you remember what Jarryca told you? Just nod if you do remember it--"

Bergas nods and lets out a hiccup for a last remaining bit of sadness that still grips him.

"I know it's hard to listen when a father tells you he knows that he has only a last few remaining days in this world. But realise this. I was purposeful in everything I've done throughout your entire life. Every action, every spoken word, every moment spent together is something you are going to remember for the rest of your life. There's one other thing to remember. Learn to know who to trust. Trust is hard-earned in the dangers of this world with the Wolf Riders endangering it. But you can trust your mother's words. They have meaning to them. Listen to them. And trust Jarryca's words, too. She is wise, and she knows there's a future for you beyond the pain you're going to endure. And whatever happens, I'll be with you still--here--"

Jerid places his hand gently on Bergas's chest over the place of the boy's beating heart.

"Whatever happens, the action of me teaching will make it feel for you like I'm still with you, Bergas. Even when in the greatest moment of despair you feel alone, you'll never be without your old father. I love you, son, and I've always been proud of you. Remember this always, no matter what happens to either of us. You have a destiny. It's something Jarryca told only me. Do you know about the War Ender?"

Bergas shakes his head.

"He's real. And he's who'll *end* the Wolf Riders. What's going to happen to you'll lead you to a man who'll begin the end of the Wolf Riders. Be brave, son, because the bad things that will happen to you, are a part of the weapon to defeat those evil men--"

CHAPTER SIXTEEN

Jerid hands Bergas one of the last small pieces of honey bread that they had in the haversack he carried. Bergas takes the bread and mechanically starts tearing small pieces from it he picks up slowly.

"Your mother once told me it was *here* she stopped for a period and that it was here she saw *you* in her own future."

Jerid swings his arm around to show the surrounding room. "She says she was frightened and alone, especially as she'd seen things in this building that no woman should see--"

She wasn't alone here. But I won't tell Bergas. If she wants him to know, she can tell it herself.

"Can we explore the building?" Bergas looks hopeful.

He's already expecting the same answer as he'd got at the previous three buildings.

"Yes, we should. Your mother said it's important you see *this* building," Jerid says.

Bergas looks at his father wide-eyed with surprise, and because he's in the middle of placing a rather large piece of bread in his mouth at the same time, the action took on a comical appearance. Jerid laughs loud seeing his son so surprise.

"What's so funny?" Bergas asks with a mouth full of bread.
"You, son, I don't think I've felt so spirited in a long time. Well, *not* since the day your mother became *my* life partner."
"I like to know about that day," Bergas blurts out.
"About when your mother and I became life partners?"
"Yes, and also about how you met her--if it's alright to ask," Bergas replies.

"Well, let's see. I *met* your mother when I was walking home. I'd just moved to the hills, where we now live--and where *your* birthing happened. If I recall, she hid behind a bush, and surprised me by speaking to me."

"Why was she hiding from you, Papa?"

"I think she didn't want people in the city to know she was seeking me out. It happens a little more than a year before you were born," Jerid answers.

"How long have you known her? Or was it *that* day you met for the first time?" Bergas continues with his questioning his father without any pauses.

"That was the first time. She told me she'd already been in the city for well over three years by then," Jerid replies, "But *never* tell that to anyone. *Not* even to Jarryca. Promise me that, son."

"I won't tell. But I think Jarryca suspects Mam has been in the city *longer*," Bergas says, then quickly adds, "But I can't tell how I know that. Please don't make me say how I know. *Please*, Papa, I can't say it or else I must break promises to you."

"If you can't tell me, then keep this information to yourself," Jerid says. He's silent for a moment, thinking deeply, before he continues speaking, "I've been thinking about what your mother has been telling me ever since the day I met her. If I keep your promise *not* to ask, then you *promise* not to repeat what I'm about to tell you, alright, son?"

Bergas swallows hard, then nods.

"I know I don't have the skill your mother possesses, and she has told me she can see things of the future. If you ask her things, always pretend that this is something you don't have knowledge of because it can be *very* dangerous for her if she has to fear your safety *too*," Jerid explains, "I sense you also have the *same* knowledge. I guessed it from certain things you told me this may be the case. For example, your mother told me that dreams matter for someone with her skills. And then you told me your dream too--"

Jerid stops talking for a moment and looks closely at his son's face to see if he understands the words just spoken. When Bergas looks up with the same fear in his eyes he'd experienced earlier in the journey, Jerid knows that Bergas comprehends what is being asked of him.

"When you ask her, and she answers you with something like 'I'll tell you soon' it isn't to keep you from knowing, but it's because it isn't time yet for it to happen. However, she never speaks of what may happen to me. Not since that night when she woke up screaming--"

"Screaming? When did that happen?" Bergas whispers.

"It happened when you were an infant, only two years old. It frightened you as well because I spent that night having to comfort both of you--"

"Is that the reason she's so reluctant about me going anywhere?" Bergas asks softly.

"Yes, but based on the many things she's said in later years, I think she *knows* more than she can tell me. I think the future is frightful for a person who knows *how* to see it. For *any* person who sees it--"

Bergas looks down quickly, realising that the last part of the words is meant for him.

"If *you* saw something happen to me in your dreams, Bergas, I don't want to know about it. I know you'll feel guilty later for *not* telling me, but if your mother is one *without* the skill she has, then that future would be *unknown* to all three of us, and it could *still* happen. But she has the skill, and I've known it for longer than you've been alive. And you, son, you got a role to play too. I heard what Draigus told you at the cave that day while he helped you, and so did your uncle. We decided that we *all* have to *trust* Jarryca--and so do you."

"He thought he spoke softly. And then I was angry with him--" Bergas whispers, feeling his eyes sting again, then adds speaking even quieter, "And then he went somewhere because I went to look for him at the harbour before we journeyed."

"He went away because your uncle and I decided that it's best to send him on the journey he has to make. The one that Jarryca showed for him to be important."

The gentleness in his father's voice makes Bergas look up. Jerid looks at eyes glistening with tears that want to start, and a face full of fear now.

"I mentioned Jarryca for a reason. And I'll never ask how you know the things she *and* your mother speak of, but that day when Hadukin came to me he had two messages. One was for you and Draigus delivered it for you, but the other was for me. Because Jarryca told Hadukin what's going to happen to *me*, and he came to swear to keep *you* safe for as long as he can. And he came to tell me, also, that Draigus is travelling to meet a man who'll free you from Wolf Riders when that comes--"

CHAPTER SEVENTEEN

"Wolf--Riders," Bergas whispers. He is now as white as moss ash and trembling with fear. His eyes dart around like any moment they can jump from the shadows in the building.

"Yes, son, wolf riders. And by *your* reaction, I now know what you've been dreaming about," Jerid says, still speaking gently.

"I thought it was just a scary dream, Papa, honest. I don't want them to take me. I don't want to lose you at sea," Bergas shrieks, now also crying uncontrollably.

In his unfathomable fear, he'd just put into words the very thing he didn't want to tell his father.

"Not--lose--*me*--" Jerid says, then he stops talking.

The sudden realisation of what his son just confessed to him jolts pain through his heart.

He knows when, and how, I'm going to die. He knows I'm going to die and that after that he's going to end up being snatched by them--

Jerid looks at his son and he sees him staring at him with both hands covering his mouth with sheer terror on his face now.

"Is that the truth you've been hiding from me all this time? Is that the reason you asked to come fishing with *me* for the last two years because... Because you saw *me* die alone, did you? You thought by coming with me you'd stop it from happening--"

Bergas nods.

"Son, there are things in the future that we cannot change--*ever*. That's something Emelyse taught me. She says one of those things was about your birthing. Alright, I'll tell you *what* she has told me about who *she* is and *what* she is, but *never* tell her I told you. And pay attention to it, because somehow I think it will become very important to you. I'm not one with *her* skill--or yours, but I've had a long life, and I helped my uncle after he told me about Jarryca and that was *long* before Emelyse came."

"Hadukin has known Jarryca for long?" Bergas almost whispers.

"Yes, son. In fact, *what* my brother did almost fifty years ago ties our family's fate to what Jarryca is, where she came from, and what she has done to get this world to be a safer place. In fact, she's from the *same* place where the Wolf Rider is from who'll rescue *you* and return *you* to your mother. You *need* to tell him you want to return home, but you *also* need to make him aware that the dreams he is experiencing, aren't simply dreams, and that they mean the words of *another* of his kind as an insult, in fact, confirm what his *real* destiny is. Jarryca told me all this."

"Is Jarryca like… Mam?"

"Before I answer that, I'm going to show you something. You need to look *well* at what I'm going to show you, because the faces of those who mean to snatch you, will be similar. If you look at them *and* recognise them, point *them* out to the Wolf Rider *from* Jarryca's town. It will set in motion *everything* to make the world safe again-- from those who'd want to bring *back* what the Warlords did."

"Warlords?"

"Yes, and come with me now--"

They both get up, and Bergas feels apprehension as he follows his father down the stairway past a painting on the wall. He glances up at it, wondering who's being depicted on that. At the bottom of the stairs, Jerid adds extra oil for the ember he holds to burn brighter. He takes Bergas's hand and walks to the dark inner corridor. He stops. He holds up the ember.

"This woman is unknown to your mother, but she feels some sort of connection to her, like she had some sort of important role in her life. You can see she was royal, but your mother thinks it's more than that. Like she said something, that binds *her* fate with what goes on *now*. That's why your mother wanted you also to see this *other* one…"

Rather forcefully, Jerid turns Bergas around to make him look at the other portrait hanging. The effect of the man's eyes has a similar effect on the boy, as it had on his mother when she saw the portrait decades earlier. Jerid feels Bergas's hand grip tighter.

"Who is he?" Bergas whispers. "He looks so evil--"

"You mother doesn't know, and I don't know either. But the retellings by the Wolf Riders will teach you *who* he is… You must listen to every one of them. You must listen to *every* word spoken. If you know what's said later on, you can help *that* Wolf Rider to understand what *his* role is. This face--is the face of an enemy so great that three thousand years later he *still* haunts this world. If you know *who* he is, you'll teach it to *that* Wolf Rider, and your mother told me it will cause one other of his kind to turn his back on this life, and be the one to stand by the War Ender's side to end all of it--"

"Who is the other man that Mam talked about when she said that?"

"She never knew, but she told me she warned him to stop chasing when he recognises the end of the Wolf Riders was beginning."

"Why don't we destroy these portraits, Papa?"

"We cannot, because its existence will convince that man that the end of the Wolf Riders will come."

"Oh, right--" Bergas says, then he's silent for a while, thinking about everything he now knows. It's almost too much to comprehend for his young mind.

But Bergas suddenly realises with clarity that he'd always known his own role in the coming events is as clear as the fact he would lose his father at sea one day.

"I think I must do it--" he mutters softly.

Jerid decides not to ask what the boy has determined. Neither does he know what Bergas thinks at that moment and frankly didn't want to know now that he knows that his fate is in death soon after they'd returned to Azaquina.

I think what I need to do is to be the most disobedient boy in all of Azaquina, and then let myself be snatched. I must pretend to be angry with my mother, and I'll miss her every day. I think I know it will be very dangerous and that I could end up never returning home. But if Jarryca is right, then I could help to end the Wolf Riders, and then no other boy will ever be snatched. I think I even know the name of the Wolf Rider Papa speaks of, but neither Papa nor Mam will ever know that--

CHAPTER EIGHTEEN

"Bergas, come to eat," Emelyse calls out loud.

A boy looks up, and he waves farewell at a few boys and girls, who surround him with, and one girl, in particular, is keen to say goodbye to him enthusiastically. He sprints fast towards a woman waiting at a higher elevation, who grins when her son rushes towards her. Bergas hugs his mother, who reciprocates the gesture with a hug of her own. When Bergas looks up, he sees a momentary sadness on her face, which she hides fast. He sees the expression on his mother's face many times in recent weeks…

It has been only a few days since he arrived back with his father. His father had fished again, but most days Bergas doesn't even ask to go with him now, and *too* often runs off towards the high hills behind his house, before his parents are awake, to avoid seeing his father's departure.

Bergas walks home holding his mother's hand, briefly waving back at his friends. One there looked sad as she waves back at him…

* * *

"Papa, can we go see the Eye of Waves tomorrow?" Bergas asks as his father sits down opposite of him.

He ignores his mother, drawing in her breath when she hears the words. It's one place Emelyse always forbade her son to see. Because very near it, lies the part of the harbour from where she'd told Jerid that Wolf Riders will snatch their son.

Jerid stares at Emelyse for a moment, then glances at Bergas, who's looking down.

Bergas can hear his mother whisper, "No, please, no, don't take him there, Jerid--"

Bergas pretends not to hear the words, but he looks up in equal shock at his father's next words. He's as pale as his mother.

"I think it's about time that we face the surrounding realities. I'm going to show him that and also the harbour, Emelyse," Jerid says coldly, "And after that, I'm going to fish again. And he's going with me every day--"

"Bergas, go to your room. I need to speak with your father alone," Emelyse says with a voice as icy cold as that of Jerid, "Go now!"

Bergas scrambles up, grabs a loaf of honey bread before running to his room, and slams his door shut. Neither parent notices the tears on his face. Neither parent realises they set in motion *his* fate and that of Jerid with their anger.

Bergas lies down on his bed and listens to his mother screaming at his father about him. But he notices something *odd* about the argument. The odd part of it is that his father is silent all the time.

I'm certain that this causes Papa to go off on his boat--, Bergas thinks.

Just as he thinks the words, a brisk gust of wind slams his window open. It startles Bergas. He looks at the window, transfixed.

That happened in my dream as well. It has begun. What Papa warned me about has begun--

Bergas knows that he will need to make out to his mother that he blames her for what will happen to his father and that he's angry, hurt and pained by the loss; a loss he'd known about for over five years ever since he had that *first* dream.

I have to remember what Papa told me when we went to look at those portraits. He angers Mam at the moment, but it's making sure that I can 'do' what Jarryca foresees. I 'have' to be snatched by the Wolf Riders. And when I'm there, I 'have' to pretend to hate it so much so 'Alagur' comes to find me--

It is the first time Bergas dares to give voice to a dream he'd been having. He knew from the words spoken between his mother and Jarryca--in a dialect that's apparently his mother's own dialect from a life *before* she came to Azaquina--that Jarryca knows the name of *that* man as well. She'd said the name, and his mother reacted like she recognised the name.

I'm certain that something more happened in her journey to this city to make her so spooked. She seems to know so much more. Papa said to me I should ask and that I'd know the truth when she tells me she tells an answer soon--

* * *

Bergas wakes up mid-morning feeling confused for a moment about *where* his father is, as he'd been told that they're going to see the Eye of Waves this day. He listens, but the entire house is silent. He straightens up in bed and looks at the open window. It hardly moved. The angry wind from the previous night had quietened down while he slept. He listens again to determine if he's truly alone or that perhaps one or both parents are still sleeping.

Bergas gets out of bed and grabs his shirt he'd thrown on the floor when he arrived in his sleeping room angrily. He looks at the window again, wondering if he should simply slip away as he'd done before, but something holds him back. He walks to the door and listens for sounds outside the sleeping room. It's still silent.

He walks through the corridor towards the front door. Reaching it, he's startled when he's spoken to, "I wondered how long it was before you'd wake up. Let's go before your mother wakes up, too. We're going to see the Eye of Waves, then you'll see what drove your mother to here. Or at least what's left over of it. And then, I'm off for my fishing journey. I don't want you to stop me going. I know it causes my demise but if there's one thing I understand of your mother's skill is that the *closer* to the here and now the event is the *less* of it a person with your mother's skill can see of it. If you saw it, it's a long time *before* it will happen still. Let's go. Put on your shoes and coat now…"

Bergas stares at his father with evident shock. It's the first time that the decisions between his parents have been different.

"Is… is… Mam not going with us?" he stutters.

"NO!"

Bergas now *knows* that the inevitable future he'd seen is in motion.

It's that one simple word from his father that seals his own fate…

CHAPTER NINETEEN

Jerid holds Bergas's hand in a firm grip. He's walking silently with all attempts for answers, that Bergas now wants, being stonewalled. Bergas glances up repeatedly at his father. Jerid refuses to look at his son, and to Bergas it feels like he's facing some sort of hefty punishment rather than what he'd hoped to be a fun day out with his father. Jerid's face is set in an angry frown which is visible on his forehead.

For a while, Bergas is only paying attention to his father, but after some fifteen minutes of walking, he notices they're avoiding the chance of being seen. Jerid isn't taking his son along the major routes around the city, but climbs up to the high mountain north of the house, and at the overhang, he turns left and leads Bergas along a narrow path only ever used by mountain sheep. Bergas has to smile for only the briefest moments when a few angry mountain sheep-- ewes in late season with their almost mature lambs--rush away from them walking past bleating their displeasure for being disturbed.

"Papa, are you angry with me?" Bergas whispers.

"No, son, I'm hurrying, so we can see it *before* your mother wakes," Jerid replies softly. "If she *still* sees us walking, she may come after us, and take you home with her. I think I worked out *where* the events she spoke of, are to happen. I'm going there to make sure *you* know where to go on *that* day--"

* * *

Bergas stares at the large rock formation below him. "That, my son, is the Eye of Waves," Jerid explains. "And if you look west of it, that's where the Temple stood--"

"The Temple?" Bergas frowns because all he sees is a pile of rocks.

"Yes, the *Temple*," another voice behind him answers.

Bergas turns in surprise to see Jarryca standing behind him, holding onto Hadukin's arm.

"Uncle Hadukin--Jarryca--why are you here?" Bergas asks in a high-pitched voice.

"Because I think you're uncertain of the future, am I right?" Jarryca answers.

Bergas's face goes bright red before nods.

"I think I'm the *only* person, other than your mother, who can answer the questions you have. But most of them *should* remain unasked until after the coming events," Jarryca scolds.

"I know what's going to happen to me--"

"I'm certain you *are*. Sit *here* with me. We will talk--*alone*," Jarryca says then she gives the two men a stern glance that speaks volumes of the authority *her* presence can still evoke in those near her. She waits until both men are gone from sight, then turns her gaze back on Bergas, who squirms in every direction under that gaze.

"Come, sit here with me, and we'll talk," Jarryca says gently. Somewhat reluctantly, Bergas complies with the request. Jarryca sits down on a boulder facing the north-west and after a few moments, Bergas sits down to her right.

"Let me start by telling you more about *that*--" she begins, "I think you'll find its retelling fascinating. Do *you* know that the Eye of Waves has existed for tens of thousands of years? All of this was once a massive cave *all* around us. That's how we got the Bay of Whispers--"

"One fisherman at the cave told me about it," Bergas whispers shyly.

"I know he did. I'm making sure as *many* learn the knowledge I have," Jarryca says softly. "But now for the *genuine* reasons I told your father to bring you *here* to meet with me--"

Bergas feels nervous suddenly, like he's done something wrong.

"I know you're experiencing dreams. No one told me. I knew it from *my* knowledge of the future. I've known since the day I asked your mother to visit me, with you along, that you'd have the *same* skill as she has. A Caller such as I can know things such as that. Do *you* know what a Caller is?"

Bergas shakes his head.

"We are people who know the future. We see the future in dreams. We also have the knowledge to see it at will," Jarryca explains. "I know there will be sadness ahead for you but much later, you'll gain a brother but not one who is born as your direct kin."

"How?"

"Because the man called Alagur will come and when he comes, he'll have a woman with him," Jarryca continues. "You need to tell your mother he's a friend. I think she'll recognise her."

"How do you know *that* name?" Bergas asks, with shock clear in his voice.

"I'm a Caller. He's part of your future. Not once, but twice. You must always remember what he asks of you before he leaves you to travel away from here--"

"What is that?"

"He'll ask you to come to where the woman comes from. She's of my kind too, but differently. She can see the past. Soon, you'll be gone from here, and you have seen this happen too. Make sure you meet this man, Alagur. He's very important for this world."

"Papa said so as well," Bergas says, then he nods.

"You're going to go to an ancient city far south of here--now filled with men riding on wolves. There will be other boys there too, but if you stand up to them, then Alagur will be the one who's going to find you. You'll know he's the man because of his wolf. Your father showed the wolves in the Northern Blades to you--yes?"

Bergas nods. "He told me about Mountain Ghost."

"Good. The name that Alagur gave his wolf when he went to get it from those mountains, is called the same name," Jarryca states, "She's going to be a friend too, even if you're going to be scared. But be wary of other men. You must tell Alagur who had taken you to the ruined city so you can assure his destiny. Can you do that?"

"I was scared before. Actually, I'm still scared, but now I know how important it all is--"

"I know you feel upset about what will happen to your father soon. He knows it's a destiny that cannot be altered. But as he told you, he'll forever be with you here--"

In a gentle gesture, Jarryca places her hand on the place where Bergas's heart beats. "He will also be here," she adds a moment later. "Your skill will grow over time, and as it does, you'll have a better grasp of the memories of him. The woman who comes will ensure that your mother tells you more about herself. Just ask, but wait for the right moment. It will come--"

CHAPTER TWENTY

The walk home is as quietly as the journey from home had been. Bergas hugs Jarryca and Hadukin before they walk down the hill with her holding onto Hadukin's arm for support. Bergas glances often back towards them.

The conversation with her had been as mysterious as the ones he'd been having with his father; none of it matches in mystery when he thinks back to the few conversations he'd listened to whenever he'd gone to the old woman's mysterious library. They spoke in a dialect not of this city but of an unknown origin which his mother seemed to speak fluently.

Bergas always pretended not to listen to it…

On this day when Bergas arrived home, there's no mother waiting for him there, waiting to embrace him.

"Remember that you cannot speak with your mother about what Jarryca told you. She'll do everything she can to shield you from the fate but that fate is set in stone and can *never* be altered."

* * *

That evening, Bergas has vivid dreams again. But he buries his face into his pillow, so not to alert his parents of dreaming in this way. This dream seems to be of him as a man in an unknown city. But his face looks happy, and he seems to walk those streets as a free man, not someone shackled into an unwanted existence as a Wolf Rider. Bergas lies awake in bed thinking about this vision. He'd understood from illicitly listening in on the conversations that his mother had been having with Jarryca, that the skill she has comes with a price. That price consists of certain knowledge that the closer you are to the actual event that the less you can see of it--if at all.

If I saw it with such ease, it's an event long way in the future--my future. If I saw myself as a free man in an unknown, undamaged city, it means that a future such as that 'will' likely happen. I just keep holding onto this dream's message, if the events that Papa mentioned to me will happen--

Bergas listens for sounds in the house, and when he hears *none* he repeats his actions of the previous evening, but this time he goes to his window and opens it. He looks up at the sky, at all the lights that blanket the night darkness. The stars there always soothe his mind whenever thoughts of the future enter his mind…

I wonder if there are others looking up at the stars tonight.

* * *

Hours later, Bergas is eating a morning meal, and he notices how *both* his parents are silent during the meal, and that afterwards his father goes off into town.

I'm sure he's gone to do his fishing as he'd stated, Bergas thinks as he watches his father go.

He does not try to ask him if he can come with him. While his father is gone, Bergas keeps looking outside to check the weather in the west--across the other side of the Bay of Whispers in the direction, where he'd seen an angry storm in his dream. He doesn't tell his mother *why* he keeps going outside, but he catches her facial expression occasionally that shows worry.

When Bergas rushes out for the eleventh time, instead of just going to check the weather, he rushes up the hill where he's certain he'd find a few of his friends playing. He stops at the fork in the path where he stops for a moment. The left path leads down to the part of the harbour where according to his father he needs to be *when* the news came…

I don't want you to die, Papa, Bergas thinks as he stares west again, *I don't want you to leave Mam and me alone in the world--*

When Bergas arrives at his friends, he tries to be as cheerful as they are. But he can't. Long before it's time for the evening meal, he trudges home, feeling a growing sadness in his heart. He's noticed only by *one* person in the group of friends, who looks after him for a long time.

Bergas sits down at the table in the front room and aimlessly draws pictures on a piece of parchment. He keeps glancing up to see if the familiar figure of his father is coming up the hill. When he sees him, he's almost tempted to rush out the house to his father, when finally he sees him walking up the hill slowly.

After another hour, he gets called to the cooking room to sit down for a meal. None of them speaks. Jerid tells nothing about his fishing trip, Emelyse never asks about it, and even the usually talkative Bergas is absolutely silent. After they eat the meal, he washes his plate without being asked, then slips to his sleeping room, and lies down on his bed fully clothed.

An hour later, when he's deep asleep, it's Jerid--and *not* Emelyse--who comes to ready him for bed, and tuck him in. The boy doesn't notice his father holding him for over thirty minutes, silently rocking him back and forth like he's an infant too scared to go to sleep.

Jerid and Emelyse sit down in the front room to talk for several hours, this time in hushed tones before they *too* go to bed in their own sleeping room, where Emelyse lies wide awake for many hours before she finally falls asleep. As soon as she sleeps, many unnatural dreams grip her mind immediately; by dreams that aren't dreams; by dreams that she thought she'd left behind when she left a dangerous city behind for good…

* * *

Emelyse wakes up startled by what happened while she slept. *The dreams have returned.*

Emelyse glances sidelong at the sleeping man next to her in the bed. She knows his fate, which has revealed itself in this dream, which isn't a normal type of dream. She can't tell him, because it will mean telling him a lot more about herself than she's done so far.

Secrets, always so many damned secrets.

She looks at the ceiling of the sleeping room, then glances at the cabinet in which she hides her secret.

After tomorrow, no one can ask about who I was or where I was from. I won't tell Bergas about myself. If he asks I'll tell him I'll tell soon--

Emelyse feels fear in her heart about what the future will bring. It's an impossible future alone with her son. And then not even for that long. She has known this since before he was even born. She will lose her son one day soon, and only to get him back because of what she'd said, all those many years ago, to a strange man whom she met in the wilderness to the east. That man will be instrumental in more ways than he'd realise.

Although I've warned him, I know that only after my son is again free from the same sort of life he is leading, that it will open his eyes to what will come next...

Emelyse glances sideways again when the man beside her grunts and then turns away from her in his sleep. She looks at him with eyes filled with love and tears. She cannot bring herself to wake him up to tell him *what* his fate will be during the following day.

But the boy stays home today because tomorrow things will start changing--

THE END

Here's how to keep in touch with me!

My website **nathaliemlromer.com**

Twitter   twitter.com/nmlromer
Facebook   facebook.com/nathaliemlromer
Blog   nathaliemlromer.blog
GoodReads   goodreads.com/nathaliemlromer
Bookbub   bookbub.com/authors/nathalie-m-l-romer

"Thank you so much for reading my book. I hope
it will give you many more years of enjoyment."

Nathalie M.L. Römer

ABOUT THE AUTHOR

Nathalie M.L. Römer was born in the Netherlands, lived there during her childhood before she moved to Curaçao as a teenager. From there, she then moved to Britain to live there for twenty-five years, before moving to Sweden where she now lives with her partner Anders.

In her childhood years and beyond, Nathalie has always loved to read novels. In her local library as a child, she would often borrow "adult audience" science fiction and fantasy novels, and as the bookworm, that she was (and still is), she would read them all in a few days... and go back for more, often. The genres that interest Nathalie the most are science fiction, fantasy and historical novels. Her favourite authors include various science fiction, fantasy and historical authors that include (but are not limited to) Isaac Asimov, Richard A. Knaak, Jean M. Auel, and Christie Golden.

In addition, to reading novels, the other interests she pursues include needlework and crafts, archaeology, reading about various science topics, home cooking, photography, web design, and playing MMO games - mostly World of Warcraft which Nathalie credits as having directly inspired her to write stories.

About the wolves in this novella!

Some aspects of how a wolf behaves in this story, have been fictionalised to fit in with the fantasy setting of the novel, however I've done much research into how these beautiful animals behave in their natural environment as well as around humans and drawing on past experiences as a dog owner, to create Yalla - who is the primary wolf to feature in the story. Some of her mannerisms are based on an Alsatian I used to own, while I also have tried to capture, how a wolf could possibly behave in nature.

Please support the various wolf sanctuary charities, that exist to give this misunderstood animal the credit it deserves!